Ellen Galford was born in New Jersey in 1947, but reversed the traditional demographic tide by emigrating to Scotland in 1971 and is now, for better or worse, a British citizen. *Queendom Come* is her third novel. Her first novel, *Moll Cutpurse: Her True History*, was published in 1984; her second, *The Fires of Bride* (1986), has recently been adapted for the stage by Red Rag, a feminist theatre group. She has worked as a television researcher and scriptwriter, edited children's books and currently writes non-fiction texts on a wide range of subjects for a large international publisher. She has lived in New York City, Glasgow and London, but has now settled in Edinburgh, in sight of the Castle, with her partner and a pair of domineering cats.

QUEENDOM COME

Ellen Galford

Published by VIRAGO PRESS Limited 1990
20–23 Mandela Street, Camden Town, London, NW1 0HQ

The right of Ellen Galford to be identified as
author of this Work has been asserted by her
in accordance with the Copyright,
Designs and Patents Act 1988.

*A CIP record for this book
is available from the British Library*

Typeset by CentraCet, Cambridge

Printed in Great Britain by
Cox & Wyman Ltd, Reading, Berkshire

This book is dedicated to the memory of my mother, Leah, who knew how to laugh

I ADMIT IT. I was conned. Go on, laugh if you want to. Just because I can whistle up winds and raise the dead doesn't mean I'm a perfect judge of character. Even Archpriestesses make mistakes.

I've had it up to here with Queens. They aren't worth the trouble. You literally move heaven and earth for them, and all they do is slap you in the face.

She tells me she wants immortality. So I set up a programme. A dream of a script. With a promise that she will arise to lead her people in their hour of need.

Is it my fault that she slept through the alarm?

Norse raids didn't wake her, nor did sieges, plagues or plots. Those disastrous defeats at Flodden and Dunbar completely passed her by. She snored through the witch-burnings – now there was a moment when she could have reappeared in a burst of vengeful and terrifying glory . . . And did she even twitch when a few rich boys sold off the rump of her ancient kingdom to the English, to pay their gambling debts? *Zzzzzzzzz*. Nevertheless, when she finally decides to stir her stumps, times are bad enough to be getting on with.

Albanna, She-Wolf of the North, may drive me up the wall, but I will grant her this: she has class and style. Take the way she makes her entrance.

It is a Saturday night like any other under the crumbling Gothic spires of Edinburgh's Royal Infirmary. In the Casualty Department, the computer terminals at the cash desks are bleeping merrily. The waiting wounded, propped up on plastic chairs, watch the video screen run yet again through the loop of aspirin advertisements. A receptionist patiently explains to a man with a knife in his neck that nothing can be done until he shows his credit cards. The nursing staff, hallucinating gently at the end of their fifty-hour shift, attend to the last of the night's intake: a grumbling appendix, eight or nine gang warfare casualties, one suspected food-poisoning, three cases of disco deafness and half a dozen more suicide attempts – quite light, really, for the time of year.

And one worn-out doctor in a rumpled white coat – her friends call her Dill, the world calls her a fool – staggers between the cubicles, trying to keep her eyes from closing. Important to preserve the illusion of competence.

'You'll never guess what's waiting in Number Three,' whispers a nurse, choking back a fit of the giggles.

'Go on, try me.' Dill's a little testy. Her sense of humour runs dry after 3 a.m.

'It's a Druid.'

'A what?'

'A Druid. You know, the old boys in the white goonies. Mistletoe and human sacrifice and all that.'

'I thought they were extinct.'

'Well, this laddie claims he's the Big Chief Heidbanger Druid. And somebody's stabbed him.'

'Where?'

'Up on Arthur's Seat. They were having some kind of ritual.'

'Not "where", Betty – WHERE?'

'Oh, sorry . . . In the bum. Nothing desperate. I've had a look and cleaned it up.' She sucks in her cheeks to hide the smile. 'He says it's a spear wound.'

Doctor and nurse avoid each other's eyes, compose their faces into masks of professional gravitas. It wouldn't do to upset the customers by laughing at them.

The Druid is lying on his side, as if attending an ancient Roman banquet, but having much less fun. Dill recognizes him, under the white hood and the affronted expression. He may be a Druid on Midsummer's Eve, but on less sacred occasions he is a Morningside estate agent. Makes a fortune out of building junior-executive deluxe starter homes on sold-off parkland, or converting damp old wash-houses into overpriced bijou maisonettes. Which is how she knows him. Seduced by his honeyed advertising copy, and squeezed by the cold realities of a seller's market, she has recently become the less-than-proud possessor of one of his properties. He shows no sign of recognition: why should he? There's one born every minute, and all punters look alike.

'Mr Melville, is it? No, don't try to get up . . .'

'I said I wanted to see the doctor in charge.'

'You've got her.'

Much to Mr Melville's mortification, Dill lifts up the druidical robes to have a look. The wound isn't very large, but it's a clean cut. Whatever made it was scalpel-sharp.

'A spear wound, you say? Are you sure?'

'Of course I'm sure,' he snaps. 'It's my – anatomy, after all.'

'Well, as it happens, it must have been a very clean spear. Who did it?'

'Are you a doctor or a detective, my dear girl? The matter has now been placed in the very competent hands of the police. Now are we going to be chatting here all night, or are you going to give me a jab so I don't expire of lockjaw?'

Not until you stop winkling old ladies out of their flats, sweetheart. And fix the dry rot you hid behind that tasteful paper on my bathroom wall. 'Of course, Mr Melville. Nurse is just away to get the vaccine.' Dill tips her a wink. Betty returns it and vanishes.

'Didn't you turn round when you felt the stab?'

'Do you think I'm daft, woman? Of course I did. There was nobody there.'

'What about the other . . . er . . . Druids?'

'The entire congregation was facing inwards, towards the centre of the sacred circle.'

'Surely someone on the opposite side of the ring saw something . . .'

'We had our eyes closed. Concentrating on the Higher Mysteries.'

'Do you think it was some sort of prank? One of your . . . um . . . colleagues . . .?'

'Absolutely out of the question. Anyway, we weren't the only people on the summit, I regret to say. These days it's like Sauchiehall Street up there on Solstice nights. Tourists. Journalists. And a pack of dishevelled women in tackety boots. Honouring the Goddess, so they say. Left-wing lesbians, if you ask me. They should flog the lot of them. *Owwww!!'*

'There we are, Mr Melville. Didn't hurt a bit. You'll live. Nurse will make up the invoice for you. Pay on the right as you go out.'

Circling the small mound at the summit of the ancient volcano, the Queen surveys her realm. She has wakened from her long sleep, opened her eyes, and taken a quick inventory of the prized possessions that surround her: sword, spear, bronze buckles, a golden torque, a slave girl and a favourite horse – the last two nothing but bones now – before pushing lightly at the crust of rock that roofs her burial chamber. Upon emerging into the cool night air, she has encountered a little band of madmen in white garments, performing some mysterious antics. Annoyed, she has identified their leader, and given him a salutary jab in the backside to drive the lesson home: sacred sites are not to be polluted.

Now the sun has risen, revealing the sweep of blue-grey water to the north and east, gilding the long ridge and the great rock that had housed one of her many forts.

For a moment she finds herself disorientated: the two lochs that once lay to the north and south of her citadel have vanished. Settlement has spread, like lichen, over the moorland. And some-thing, something she can't quite put her finger on, is different. She looks southwest, to the cluster of great hills, and southeast, over rolling farmlands, towards the distant boundary between her own tribe and the untrustworthy clans of the South. Then she realizes what's missing: the unbroken expanses of oak, elm, birch and pine are gone. Someone has mislaid the ancient forest of Drumselch. She shakes her head. Where does the present ruler go when it's time to hunt and kill the sacred stag?

Having allowed herself to fall somewhat out of touch with current affairs, she wonders what sort of world she has come into. Well, I have news for her . . .

*

We are in the third decade of the Blue Reich, somewhere in the declining days of the Hanoverian dynasty. Across the nominal border and far to the South, Parliament has been busy doing its mistress's bidding. The latest in its sequence of mould-breaking legislation is the new Sexual Normality Bill, passed this very night by a House full of adulterers, voyeurs, fetishists and secret spankers. The leaders of the various Loyal Oppositions, for once, have little to say on the matter. The issue is not a vote-getter.

The PM whisks away from the House, satisfied with the evening's business, to play hostess at an important cultural event. The Bond Street saleroom hums with the excitement of another stunningly successful auction of surplus government real estate. Sleek-suited businesspersons of all nationalities discreetly lift their wafer-thin platinum calculators, twitch their catalogues or simply nod to nudge the bidding up to unprecedented heights. Not since the coal-mines were sold off as private wine cellars has there been such an enthusiastic response from the international investment community.

'Lot forty-six. The Callanish Stones. One extensive megalithic monument with remnants of chambered cairn, situated in remote location on Hebridean island of Lewis. Excellent sea views, recently freed of planning controls, would make ideal site for luxury holiday development or imaginative conversion into large private shooting lodge. Let us start the bidding at three million . . . three million . . . three five . . . four . . . four five . . . five . . . five five . . . Excuse me, sir, bearded gentleman in the front row, was that a bid, sir? . . . Very good . . . Six . . . seven . . . bid with the house at seven-five . . . any advance on seven-five . . .? . . . Wait, telephone bid from Tokyo for eight and a half . . . nine . . . nine-five . . . nine-seven . . . ten . . . ten-five, eleven . . . are you finished bidding, Rome? Thank you . . . Twelve, thirteen . . . any more . . . at thirteen . . .' (Bang!) 'Thirteen it is. Sold at thirteen million pounds to the representative of KTR Properties . . .'

'Lot forty-seven. Stirling Castle. Centrally located hilltop site with first-rate motorway connections . . . ideal for shopping complex, time-share development or theme park . . .'

At the sale's conclusion, the chosen few are discreetly ushered upstairs to a private room for a champagne reception.

'Well done!' purrs the PM to the Scottish Colonial Governor. 'Your illustrated catalogue was a triumph. The aerial close-up shots were most effective. However did you manage them?'

'Easy. Our chaps from the RAF. They're roaring over that ground twenty times a day on their low-altitude training flights. Simply point a camera while they ruffle the fleece on a few sheep, and Bob's your uncle!'

'Another sale as good as this one, and we'll be able to drop the capital gains tax altogether. I hope you've assembled your list of items for the next round.'

'The details will be on your desk first thing Monday morning.'

'I presume that sea-loch up in the far northwest is on it . . . You know. The one we spoke about, with the unpronounceable name . . .'

'With all due respect . . . I'm still a little worried about putting that one forward . . .'

'Nonsense! It would make a superb site for a marina. And the Americans are very interested in quarrying the hill . . .'

He drops his voice to a level well below the party's cheerful hubbub. 'But what about the flasks, ma'am?'

'What flasks? Oh, those. They're buried miles offshore . . .'

'But what if they really are leaking . . .?'

'Don't tell me you of all people are falling for those silly rumours. There is absolutely no evidence thus far . . . Just because a few dozen shepherds and fishermen have sprouted extra thumbs is no reason to jump to any conclusions . . . For all we know it could be due to sunspot activity. Or to all that porridge they eat up there . . .!'

'But if a connection did emerge, after the sale went ahead, couldn't we be sued by the purchaser for . . .?'

She throws him a look that says another word will be more than his job's worth.

'Stop fussing! When we write the description of that site in the auction catalogue, we simply make sure to mark the lot "As Seen". That covers everything. Besides, it's only going to be some foreigner who buys up the site, in any case. Who else has that kind of money to throw about? Caveat emptor is what I say. It's the law of the market.'

Meanwhile, back in Albanna's former realm, Dr Marion Dillon finishes her shift at the Royal Infirmary, unaware that she has just been declared Illegal. Her first act is to sleep for fourteen hours. Her second is less prudent. She goes to a party.

She puts on the only thing she can find that's clean – a well-faded pair of Levis, of considerable antiquarian interest – and waltzes off to her friend Lilias's new house at the top of a yet-to-be-improved tenement up the road from the Commonwealth Pool. One of the very few that the property developers haven't got to yet. A haunt of students and other marginalia, where every flat on the stair has eleven names on the door.

Dill's friend Lilias has sunk every penny of her twenty years' redundancy money into buying it, and now that they've closed down the Social Work Department she has plenty of time to fix the place up. She'll need it.

'Oh shit, not again!!' is her greeting, as the door falls off its hinges. 'Never mind. I've always wanted to find out how to rehang doors. I'm learning a lot. Did you know you can cure dry rot with sesame oil and natural yogurt?'

The party, like Lilias, is very well organized. Neatly lettered signs announce COATS IN HERE; TOILET CHAIN BROKEN – PLEASE USE BUCKET TO FLUSH; DRINKS THIS WAY; FOOD – VEGAN; FOOD – ORDINARY VEGETARIAN; NON-SMOKING AREA BEYOND THIS POINT BEWARE MISSING FLOORBOARDS!!!

Dill nods to the group of gay men standing conspicuously in the hallway. Single-sex gatherings have attracted police attention for some time now. These days, no party is complete without a few token opposites.

Inside, her eyes adjust to the candlelit gloom to discover several dozen familiar faces and a few unknowns: the inevitable Australian backpackers in search of old world culture, a brace of visiting American academics here for short-term research (who else could afford the library fees?), the usual band of jaded veterans, a new crop of baby dykes, plus the entire all-star cast of the banned crypto-feminist musical comedy *Pigs Will Fly*, who have just finished their prison sentences for contravening the Official Viewpoints Act.

Dill kisses and hellos her way through the crowd to the wide bay window, where she has spotted a familiar back, swathed in an old lace tablecloth. Its owner is contemplating Arthur's Seat, which seems close enough to touch in the strong light of a June evening.

'Nice view, eh? Now I see why Lilias wanted this dump.'

'Well, if it isn't Dr Marie Cure-all.' Shona's amber eyes, kohl-fringed, turn towards her, pomegranate-painted lips part in a smile. Strings of beads click and clatter. 'I don't need to ask how you're doing, chookie-birdie. I can tell. Your aura is practically colourless.'

'Heaven forfend. Is that fatal?'

'It could be. If you don't take rapid restorative measures.'

'Any suggestions?'

'Do you mind? I'm in the alternative healing business now. I normally charge for this sort of advice.'

'Well, don't expect me to congratulate you. You know my line on all that tripe.'

'It's all right for you, Doctor, with those little letters after your name. You're set up for life. But what else am I supposed to do with a half-completed doctorate in Early Celtic Studies? I'll be paying back my student loans till I'm ninety-seven.'

'What happened to your restaurant job?'

'They had to close down. The chef's gone into sanctuary.'

'Sanctuary?'

'He's a political refugee. And the Home Office wants to swap him back to the dictatorship in exchange for some English gun-runner.'

'That's terrible. Whatever happened to justice? And how do I live without his garlic soup?'

'Just now he's hiding out in the vestry of a church down in Leith. You know, the one that used to do the jumble sales for the Peace Movement before they banned it. There's only a small gas ring and a pocket knife to work with. But he seems to be acquiring a coterie of appreciative sympathizers. I'm sure that a small bribe – or a contribution to the Roof Repairs Fund – would secure you a table in a few weeks' time.'

'Sounds wonderful. Just the thing for my aura. But will I last out that long?'

'I'll do you a trade. You tell me what to do for my cystitis – seeing that my preferred treatment of meditation, flower remedies and acupuncture has failed me, just this once – and I'll devise you a course of spiritual refreshment and restoration. Free and gratis.'

'For the sake of my poor benighted aura, you have a deal.'

Dill tells Shona what to do about her southern hemisphere, with various caveats, options and personal recommendations. 'Right. That should sort you out. If it's no better in a week, ring me. Now what about my poor old aura?'

'I shall ponder.'

Shona turns back to the window.

'Look at that hill,' she says. 'That's one bloody great cosmic generator . . .'

Dill's attention wanders. She has heard Shona sing this song before.

'You should have been with us last night. The vibes up there were unbelievable.'

Dill's attention comes home again. 'On Arthur's Seat? Last night?'

'Where else do true believers go to praise the Lady of Light, my dear? It was the Solstice – or didn't you know?'

'Tell me about it . . . Who was there? Did you see anything strange? Don't leave anything out.'

'Goodness me. I thought you were the person who dismissed all this stuff as leftover countercultural claptrap . . .'

'Well, I was. And I am. And I do . . . but last night, something turned up in Casualty . . .' Dill launches into the tale of the Druid with the punctured bottom.

Shona places a ring-laden hand on Dill's sleeve. 'Wait a minute. This music is driving me up the wall. Just how desperate are you to stay at this party?'

Dill looks around the room. And sees someone she'd rather not run into. An early indiscretion back in town. 'Not very.'

'Why don't we go for a little stroll up the hill? There'll be light for ages yet. I'll tell you what I saw last night – and you can get a good healthy blast of earth-energy at the same time.'

'Let's do it.'

They wave their thanks to Lilias and slip away, inspiring the first new gossip of the summer season.

Dill is impressed. Shona glides up the steep path without effort, while she has been forced to stop three or four times on the pretext of admiring the view.

'Great, eh? If we hadn't had that bunch of bampots running about with their socks and sandals, it would have been truly world-shaking up here last night.'

'You mean the Druids?'

'I mean the Mystic Brotherhood of Suburban Dentists. They think they own this place. Come up twice a year on the great festivals with their gear stowed in House of Fraser carrier bags, and dance about performing ancient rites that go back at least as far as 1926. They don't like us much.'

'Who's Us?'

'The Sisterhood, daftie. A party of like-minded Amazons who wish to warm our toes on the ley lines and pay our respects to the Goddess on appropriate holy days.'

'Anyone I know?'

'Inevitably.'

'Let me guess . . . Janet . . .?'

'Are you joking? That weekend Wicca? She's far too busy investing the profits from her Astrology Shop in South African gold shares, or somesuch . . .'

'I take it you two aren't lovers any more.'

She flicks Dill a pitying glance. 'Oh, sweetieheart, you *are* out of touch.'

'Now about last night . . .'

'Well, as I was saying . . . The Boys' Brigade was right scunnered when they came puffing up the last bit of path and found us already in command of the bit with the cairn at the top. You should have heard the things they called us. We just ignored them . . . we were trying to get in touch with the Higher Energies, and all, and weren't about to break the magic with a rammy. Except for Wee Agnes. She wanted to have a go at them. We had to hold her back. For a vegetarian, she's awful ready with her fists . . .'

'Wee Agnes? You're joking. She's just been promoted. Queen of the Physio Department. I'll have to take the piss out of her next week in the staff canteen.'

'I wouldn't, if I were you. She finally made fourth dan black belt in her karate class.'

'Wherever does she find the time?'

'Stop interrupting. I'll fill you in on the gossip later. Do you want to hear what happened last night, or don't you?'

'Sorry.'

'That's better. Anyway, we manage to calm down Aggie . . . Meanwhile, the usual bunch of hack photographers and insomniac tourists are swarming all over the slope, hoping the Druids will do a human sacrifice or something, I suppose. So we're hanging on to the cairn, right at the top, and the boys in white are building their barbecue or whatever down on the open bit – just over there . . . We forget all about everything, and really get into our chanting. And then I get sort of disorientated. I keep thinking there are six of us in the circle instead of five . . . Now don't you be spooked, Shona, I tell myself, we're safe in the lap of the Mother. Then one of the Druids starts screaming. We all jump sky-high – nearly fell off the bloody hill. They look up in our direction, pointing and shaking their heads. I swear they'd have had us done for GBH if we hadn't all been way over on the other side, with dozens of witnesses to swear we were chanting away in good style. I'm not joking, Dill, we were generating some serious power. Practically levitating. Then that bauchle goes bananas. Totally broke the spell. Bastard!'

The rest is as Dill has heard it in Casualty from Mr We-Can-Get-You-A-Mortgage-No-Problem Melville.

'He insisted it was a spear wound. I've never actually seen one, but I suppose it could have been . . .'

'If you ask me, the chappie guzzled too much usquebaugh and sat down hard on a jaggy stone.'

'He claimed he was standing up at the time.'

They climb to the summit, right on the stony head of the great crouching lioness. 'They say this is the place', whispers Shona, 'where folk used to come to meet the Devil.' Dill tells her to shut up. As spiritually sensitive as a pair of old welly boots, even she can smell the strangeness.

In the fading light, they see cars moving on the road through the park below, but no sound rises, except the gathering wind.

'Great place for a fortress,' says Dill, intent on breaking the mood. 'You could see the enemy coming from any direction.'

'Unless', murmurs Shona, 'they came out of the hill itself.'

'I wish you hadn't said that.' Dill thinks about getting her eyes tested. Something that has no right to be there is now hovering behind Shona's left shoulder.

'Shona . . . did we smoke anything at that party?'

'Of course not. We were in the non-smoking room.'

'Then I think I'd like to start running now.'

'Me too.'

Dill has not been famous for speed and agility. At school she was the despair of her Physical Education teachers. For ten years she has told patients to take more exercise, and resolutely ignored her own advice. But now she flies down the stony path with all the agility of an amphetamine-crazed gazelle, following every twist and bend without an instant's hesitation, although the light is now completely gone. Shona is close behind, almost leapfrogging over her, and something else – silent but very fast – is following Shona.

At this juncture, it is probably best to provide a little light relief and return to the government.

Down South in the imperial capital, lights burn late at Downing Street. They are putting the finishing touches to the Public Flogging of Offenders Bill. A special Cabinet subcommittee is reviewing the technology.

'Birch?'

'Rather scarce, alas, since the Great Hurricane.'

'Surely not extinct. Hard to beat it for the purpose.'

'Oh, it can be bought. But the price is out the window. Let's not burst the budget.'

'Understood.'

'What about a bola?'

'What?'

'Thong with weights on the end. Gauchos use 'em.'

Around the table, breaths are sharply taken in.

'Argentinian? Never! We must buy British! . . .'

'Perhaps not. Forget I mentioned it. Cat-o'-nine-tails?'

'And have those animal rights fanatics down on us again . . .?'

'With all due respect, ma'am, I don't think you quite understand. It isn't actually a cat, in fact, it's a . . .'

'Forget facts. I said No.'

'But . . .'

A warning look. A short but profound silence. The gentle rustling of an imminent Cabinet Reshuffle?

'Be that as it may,' purrs the Secretary of State for Style, oiling the choppy waters for the agenda's sake, 'the main problem with the cat is that it has too much of a period feel to it. Press gangs and Captain Bligh and all that. You know what I mean.'

'Frankly, I don't. History, I'm glad to say, was not Our subject.'

'Quite right, too. An untidy field. In any case, I rather think we should be aiming at a more forward-looking, contemporary image, don't you, Prime Minister?'

'I hope I should not construe that as an attack on Traditional Values.'

There is a moment's respectful silence.

'Got it, by Jove!' The crisply curled Caledonian syllables snap from the lips of the Scottish Colonial Governor.

'Ye-e-es?'

'Lochgelly!'

'What?'

'Who?'

'Eh?'

'Wot?'

'Do explain yourself, man.'

'Lochgelly. The tawse. The leather peril. Imprinting messages of moral rectitude and careful grammar upon the upturned palms of generations of Scottish schoolchildren. Excellent medicine for the thick and the idle. It was a sad day when our unlamented predecessors banned its use.'

'Lock – what did you say?'

'Lochgelly.'

'Pardon me, old chap,' says the Defence Supremo, who goes North every year for a spot of shooting. 'But isn't Lochgelly up your way somewhere?'

'Quite right. A broken-down relic from the prehistoric Coal Age. In darkest Fife. In its long-gone heyday, the place did not depend solely on the mines for its livelihood. To its credit, it boasted other industries. Notably the manufacturing of the aforesaid flexible leather straps – in a variety of weights and sizes. Generations of Scottish schoolmasters, employing a well-known device of classical rhetoric, used the place of origin as an affectionate sobriquet for this handy little ally.'

'How very interesting. And do they still make these articles up there in . . . Loch . . . jelly?'

'I think not. Unfortunately, the market dried up. All those woolly pink liberal views about sparing the rod . . .'

'Perhaps we could stimulate a revival of this ancient craft, so traditional and yet so relevant to modern needs.'

'A first-rate idea. The Scots are always whingeing on about unemployment. Well, here's some ready-made job creation for them.'

'Not to mention a very promising export market.'

'The factory might still be there, for all we know. Not much changes in Lochgelly.'

'Why not send up a working party?'

'I'll volunteer. One gets a jolly good game of golf up there this time of year.'

A pause for thought. The Prime Ministerial Consort is an aficionado of the sport. 'You know, I can't stress often enough how important it is for us to show the flag in the outer regions from time to time.' She beams at her courtiers. 'Let's all go.'

A spear sings through the air and lands an inch from Dill's left foot. Behind it, a shouted command, in an incomprehensible tongue, is nevertheless unmistakably: 'Freeze, I've got you covered!'

Well schooled in old Westerns, they put up their hands and turn round, very slowly.

The woman who confronts them, brandishing a sword, is barely five feet tall. Thick ropes of oiled black hair, plaited with red ribbons, dangle over her shoulders, three on either side. Her tattooed face is daubed with blue paint, in elaborate patterns, and her teeth are blackened. She wears some kind of long tunic, silver armbands, and half a dozen strings of beads. Thonged sandals expose well-calloused toes, with nails as long and curved as talons. And the smell that wafts towards them is not to be believed.

Menacing her captives with the sword, she retrieves her spear, then launches into an elaborate monologue, apparently ending with a set of questions. When they look at her blankly, she stamps her foot and repeats what seems to be the same inquiry.

Dill shakes her head and shrugs her shoulders, miming an abject apology.

The woman grits her teeth and makes a third attempt, raising her voice to a near shout and enunciating every syllable.

'Typical,' mutters Dill. 'She must be English.'

'Shut up!' Shona is unamused by Dill's brave attempt at humour under fire. She is beckoning to the stranger, cupping one hand behind her ear, and miming a plea to the woman to repeat her words, just one more time.

Fear and shock, Dill surmises, have driven her friend over the edge. Here they stand, menaced by a gabbling apparition with a very real spear, and all Shona can do is play Charades.

Exasperated, the woman repeats the question.

'Maybe I'm round the twist, Dill, but I think I know what she's saying. It sounds like some kind of early Gaelic – with a bit of Latin thrown in. Extraordinary accent.'

Their captor jabs the air with her spear.

'Forget the linguistics tutorial. Try to talk to her.'

Syllable by syllable, Shona speaks the same words back, then adds a tentative phrase of her own.

The woman nods vigorously, her eyes wide and frantic.

'Did you get it?'

'You're not going to believe this . . .'

'Try me.'

'She wants to know where she can go for a pee. Somewhere that isn't sacred ground.'

Shona ventures a few Gaelic words of her own. The woman looks relieved.

'What did you say?'

'I said we'd go to your place. It's closer than mine. And it definitely isn't holy.'

The spirits must be smiling. For the first time in living memory, a taxi appears the moment it is needed. If Dill were not so narrow-minded she would now perceive the intervention of some Unseen Power.

'Morningside, and hurry, please.'

'Been to a costume party, girls?' the driver asks, and never gives them a second glance.

They arrive at an imposing Victorian villa, turreted and gabled in the Scottish baronial style ('Select residential district, close to all amenities'). Bypassing the handsome front door, Dill leads her guests round to the back of the house and into a small outbuilding that was home to assorted copper wash boilers until Mr Melville sent round his minions with a few sheets of plasterboard and some tins of pastel paint. It is, as always, freezing: there is central heating, of a sort ('fully modernized, to a high standard'), but most of the warmth goes out through the ill-fitting windows. They escort their terrifying guest into the tiny bathroom ('new ultramodern luxury avocado-coloured suite'). She stares about her, bemused, until Shona points to the toilet. Greeted by a blank look, Shona makes a virtue of necessity and demonstrates its use. The woman's next gesture needs no translation: she requires privacy. They back away.

'Who or what do you think she is?'

'Heaven knows. But I think I can guess who stabbed our friendly local property developer.'

'He certainly deserved it,' says Shona, tracing the progress of the new crack in the sitting-room wall.

'So what do we do now?'

'I imagine she'll be the one to tell us.'

'Can you really understand her?'

'Well, I got her this far, didn't I? It's a very archaic form of the

Gaelic, I think. Imagine what we can learn from her. This could be the resurrection of my academic career . . .'

'Speaking of resurrection, do you think she . . .'

'Just don't say it, Dill. I can't deal with anything like that. It's too heavy.'

'I thought you were the one who liked to commune with the Higher Mysteries.'

They jump at the sound of the toilet flushing.

'She certainly learns fast . . .'

This is followed, in rapid succession, by the noise of sink taps, extractor fan, bath and shower, accompanied by shrieks of outrage.

'Well, maybe not . . .'

The visitor appears in the doorway, with water dripping from hair and spear and a very baleful expression. She mutters something; Shona asks her, very respectfully, to repeat it.

'What did she say?'

'She says that relieving oneself inside a building is a filthy habit.'

The lady's next statement is unambiguous. She points to her mouth and her stomach.

'Oh God, there's not a crumb in the house.'

'Well, I'll go for a carry-out. Make her a cup of tea or something. And can you lend me some money? I'm afraid I'm skint.'

She turns to her guest and explains, with the aid of sign language, that she is going out to hunt for food.

Dill hands her a ten-pound note.

'Better make it twenty. The poor dear's ravenous. Says she hasn't eaten a thing for over a thousand years.'

'I assume that is something of an exaggeration.'

'Well, if you knew anything about the old bardic tradition, you'd understand that poetic hyperbole was characteristic of early Celtic style.'

The woman looks impatient, barks a command, and shakes her spear.

'Does your academic background give you any clue about what she'd like to eat?'

'Whatever Morningside Road can offer at this hour, Goddess preserve us, will have to do.'

She abandons Dill to the mercies of her guest.

Dill mimes the offer of something to drink. The woman follows her into the cubbyhole of a kitchen ('charming, all-electric luxury kitchenette') and watches every move she makes. Dill offers the entire contents of her refrigerator: a carton of orange juice, another of semi-skimmed, long-life milk and a can of low-calorie Irn Bru. Dill proffers a glass, and the woman samples each one in turn, then mixes herself a cocktail of all three. She drinks deep, nods, and thrusts the mixture back at Dill. Afraid to defy her (one hand still rests lightly on the sword at her hip), Dill drains the glass with enthusiastic gestures of approval.

She wanders around the room, studying the vintage collection of 1970s lesbian feminist posters.

'Take a good look, sister. Those are collectors' items. No longer allowed to be sold or displayed in public places.'

Dill can't think of anything to say in sign language. Her face aches from diplomatic smiling. She wonders if Shona has done a bunk.

Uncharitable thoughts. But the cavalry soon rides over the hill, carrying an aromatic collection of bags and boxes.

'Just to be safe, I got her some of everything. A fish supper from the chippie, chicken tikka from the Indian, a take-away pizza, and an order of Chinese spare ribs.'

'What if she's a vegetarian?'

'Somehow I don't think so.' She nods towards the Amazon, who has torn open the wrappings and is now spearing chunks of chicken tikka on the point of an ornate dagger. With an imperious gesture, she bids them sit down and share her feast.

'I don't think she'd like it if we refused.'

They receive their first lesson in ancient Celtic table manners. The secret is this: if someone with a dagger reaches for the last slice of pizza just as you do, back off gently and settle for a chip.

Dill carries the empty containers into the kitchen. Shona squeezes in behind her.

'What now? You're the expert.'

'Perhaps propose a bath? She's a bit high, isn't she?'

'That's an understatement. What do you suggest – you hold her down, and I'll disarm her and rip her clothes off? Easy.'

They are summoned back to the sitting-room by the imperious chink of a knife against glass.

The woman rises, strikes a formal, declamatory pose, and speaks:

> 'Sweeter than the salmon caught in the nets of the Black
>   River,
> More savoury than bannocks baked on the hearth of
>   Morag Mhor,
> More nourishing than the milk of the Great Brindle Cow
> Are your gifts to me, O Strangers.'

What? Yes. You heard it. They didn't believe it either.

She stops, and looks expectant.

What else can they do? They applaud until their hands hurt.

'You're speaking English.'

'Is that what you call it? And why shouldn't I? I have eaten your food.'

The logic of this escapes them. Strictly speaking, if that's how it works, the lady should now be using a mixture of Italian, Chinese and Gujarati.

'Would you mind if we asked you . . .?'

She cuts them short, her hand back again on the sword hilt. 'I do the asking here.'

She means it. Whoever she is, she has the habit of command. She would remind Dill of a Chief Nursing Officer, if it weren't for those grimy fingernails.

She begins the interrogation, barking out her questions like a drill sergeant.

> 'What year is this?'
> 'Who is your ruler?'
> 'What is the name of your tribe?'
> 'Where is the battlefield?'
> 'Where are your priestesses?'
> 'Who holds the Castle of the Maidens now?'
> They gawp. She grows angry.
> 'Don't you know who I am?'

25

Dill shakes her head, with a self-deprecating smile. Shona shrugs her shoulders and looks nervous.

'I am Albanna!' She waits, arms folded on her chest, for a response.

'I have come back to you!'

Their blank looks enrage her. She raises her sword. 'On your knees!'

They fall to the foam-backed carpet. She looks from Shona to Dill, then back again, as if wondering whom to kill first. Then the light breaks.

'You don't know who I am? You really don't?'

They shake their heads in unison.

'I can't believe it.' She reaches out, grabs Shona by the string of beads round her neck, pulls her close and looks deep into her eyes. 'Do you swear it – by the clitoris of your grandmother?'

Shona flinches. Clearly she never imagined her grandmother had one.

'Well . . .?'

'I swear.'

'Me too.'

'Honestly. We're terribly sorry, but we don't know who you are.'

'Didn't you know that I was coming? Were there no signs, no portents?'

'Like what?'

'No double moons? No rainstorms of flower petals? No noontime disappearances of the sun?'

'Not that I've noticed,' says Dill. 'But then I work nights.'

She turns to Shona – who is, after all, as she never tires of reminding people, closely attuned to the movements of the planets and the pulse of the Universe.

'Well, there has been something very strange happening in the fourth house of Mercury . . . And, come to think of it, my cats have been walking widdershins round their food bowl, and . . .' She begins to hit her stride. 'And I know I dreamed about flying upside down last week, and . . .'

Albanna sighs. 'I seem to have fallen amidst ignorant savages.'

'Now, just a minute . . .'

She glares. 'Silence. Queens do not brook interruptions. In a time before your time,' she intones, 'I was the Queen of all this land, and far beyond it. And when I died, it was promised that I would return in a time of trial and trouble, when my people had need of me. My name would be a beacon of hope, shining down through the generations. And now you tell me you don't even know who I am!'

Distracted, she tears at her tightly wound plaits. 'That wretched Gwhyldis should be rent limb from limb and flung into the sea!'

Dill takes a breath and ventures in. 'If it is any comfort to you, O Mighty Queen,' she offers, shifting from one stiff knee to the other, 'you have indeed turned up in a time of trial and trouble. Things are fairly dreadful just now, one way and another.'

Albanna ponders this. 'This is not at all what I was led to expect. But if things are bad, it may be Gwhyldis did not completely fail me. Perhaps I shall only cut off one of her arms when next we meet.'

'Begging Your Highness's indulgence . . .' Shona is getting into the way of things now. 'Who is Gwhyldis?'

'The greatest priestess in the realm. No magic is beyond her powers. Or so I thought until this little cock-up. Nevertheless, it is proof of her skill that I stand before you now. And when I find her, I shall make her suffer for the breakdown in arrangements.'

'When you find her?'

'If I have succeeded in crossing the ages and making my Return, you can be sure that Gwhyldis will be around here somewhere.'

She's right, of course. I could hardly trust her to handle the situation on her own. Her kind are, after all, used to sitting back while other people do the work. So it was necessary that I should turn up in the same place at precisely the same moment. This is where I made a tiny error in my calculations. I blame it on all these satellites transmitting military secrets and television game shows. The air is full of noises.

CHAPTER TWO

THE FORMULA I DEVELOPED was supposed to deposit me in the very epicentre of Blue Reich power. Instead, I find myself in the middle of a crumbling ex-council scheme on Edinburgh's outskirts. I appear to be in sole charge of a pair of three-year-old twins. The same slip-up that has brought me into their lives has removed their mother. But do not grieve for them – or her. The result of one night of disappointing passion with an almost famous guitarist, their arrival put paid to her career as a chanteuse. She never liked them much; her lullabies, though in perfect pitch, were sung through gritted teeth. Anyway, as a result of our accidental life-swap, she has been conveyed to my own time and place, where she will win wealth and stardom belting out post-punk war chants and torchy ballads in the style of Piaf.

Of course I could have undone the damage, but I decide to stay put. The small squealing persons turn out to be identical females. Tribes less enlightened than our own would have strangled both of them at birth, and slipped the alarmingly matched pair of bodies into the nearest bog. But among my people, twins – especially when female – are welcomed as gifts from the Goddess.

Encouraged by such a good omen, I survey my new head-quarters: a semi-derelict flat, damp as a mushroom. I investigate all handles, knobs and taps, explore drawers and cupboards, make a few witty spells, and fill the house with light and colour.

I have never claimed a shred of maternal instinct, but I don't see why someone who can tap dance to the music of the spheres shouldn't penetrate the mysteries of motherhood. Within a day or two I know how to cook fish fingers, and can steer the double pushchair with the skill of a charioteer. Only in moments of extreme duress, such as children's bedtime, do I call upon my higher powers. Once, pressed beyond all endurance, I turn a Poll Tax Collector into a small brown dog. And, of course, I keep an eye on things over in Morningside.

Shona, sworn to secrecy, has sailed off into the sunset: it is time for her rebirthing workshop. She leaves Dill holding the metaphorical baby, who demands frequent refills of Irn Bru, plus a detailed report on the current state of her realm. She drinks in both with equal avidity, and the gloomier the news, the better she seems to like it.

'So,' says Dill, weary after an all-night trip down the more sordid alleyways of Memory Lane, and a foolhardy attempt at some do-it-yourself political analysis, 'it all sort of crept up on us. One damned thing after another. Every time we said They Wouldn't Dare, they made a few placatory noises, and then they went ahead and did it. It stopped being a joke a long time ago. But the full horror didn't really hit home until the news came from America about Billie Blossop . . .'

'Billie Blossop?'

'Celebrated right-on folksinger. Madonna of the Whales. The Green Movement's answer to Vera Lynn. We heard that she had cut short her concert tour of Latin American guerrilla camps and rushed back to California to record a special album. She called it "A Song for Britain". That's when we knew we were really in the shit.'

'Right,' says Albanna after a pause for thought, 'bring me my sword and shield. I'm off. Your prayers are answered, O my people. Your Queen has returned to save you.'

Before departing, she rewards Dill for her hospitality with the customary mark of royal favour. I know it well, but Dr Dillon may be a little surprised. Somehow I don't think your current monarch salutes her subjects with a long, lingering kiss and an appreciative pat on the bottom. By the time Dill shuts her mouth again, Albanna has vanished.

I know where she's headed. In search of the people who really run things. She needn't have troubled: they'll soon find her.

*

Dill's friend Shona, virtually penniless, barters for life's small necessities. She visits her astrologer four times a year, and cooks her supper in exchange for a consultation. She washes floors for her aromatherapist, babysits for the woman who reads her aura, and tends the garden for the formidable lady who sorts out her psyche. With all of these her relationship transcends the purely professional, and every contact concludes with a gossip and a cup of tea. So she never knows whether it is the stargazer, the aura-detective or the woman with herbal oil on her hands who first passes on the story of Albanna. It is not impossible, after all, that one (or more?) are government agents; the tentacles of the State, in these days of databases, probe far and deep.

By whatever means, the interesting piece of information wends its way within a matter of hours to the Scottish Office, and swiftly on to Downing Street. Small, unminuted meetings are held, a few trusted specialists consulted and sworn to secrecy, and the hunt is on.

Thanks to her tattoos and queenly garments, the lady makes it easy for the authorities to track her down. Among the shoppers in Princes Street, locals intent on the summer sales and tourists in search of ancestral tartans, she is easily spotted and swiftly extracted from the crowd. No force is necessary: an unmarked van pulls up in front of Marks and Spencer, disgorges a woman and a man in dark sunglasses who fall to their knees in gestures of awe and homage. Albanna extends her hands to be kissed, and is drawn – ceremoniously, but at top speed – into the vehicle. Someone, somewhere, has been exceptionally well briefed on Proto-Pictish protocol.

The disappearance of her house-guest is the last thing on Dr Dillon's mind. The next morning, when she arrives at work, a secretary summons her into the office of the Hospital Administrator.

'We can't discriminate between men and women.'

'I'm relieved to hear it,' says Dill, bemused.

'And that's why we have to let you go.'

The Assistant Human Resources Manager of Scothealth plc – new owners of the Royal Infirmary – has a face from which all expression has been washed and ironed. He is used to these sessions; Dill is not.

'What?'

'What I said. Perverts – male and female – are now regarded as a health risk.'

'You can't be serious.'

'We don't joke about That Disease. Whether your particular – ah – sexual habits are high or low risk is quite irrelevant. A deviant is a deviant. We owe it to our customers to protect them. Management policy, I'm afraid. And you know what the new law says about the removal of your employment rights. I'm afraid you'll have to go.'

Dill observes that any heterosexual is a greater risk than she is, and begins revving up for an outburst of Krakatoan intensity.

'You'd do well to avoid a fuss, Dr Dillon. If you pack up and go quietly, I'll see what I can do about keeping the reason for your dismissal off the records.'

It turns out that they are closing down the entire hospital. The buildings occupy a prime piece of city-centre real estate; the new management regards their present use as a criminal waste of assets. Dill's sacking, one of the first to take advantage of the Employment Clause in the shiny new Sexual Normality Act, is simply a canny ploy to avoid paying her redundancy money.

Most of her colleagues are unworried. They are well aware that Adam Smith Mutual, just up the road, is recruiting a large team of medical assessors for its Executive Health Insurance Plan. Dill does not even bother to apply. She knows full well that all insurance companies subscribe to the Central Employee Vetting Index. And, sure as eggs are eggs, her card is marked.

But she will not take this lying down. For old times' sake, she decides to bring the matter to the Amalgamated Health Workers' Union. Oh yes, there is still a union. But its role in the present set-up has withered to something like that of a vestigial tail.

The organizing secretary sits in his small office in the basement of a closed-down antenatal clinic, surrounded by posters of old benefit concerts for Latin American resistance struggles.

'That's a shame, comrade. Really terrible.'

'Anything you can do?'

'I'd like to help, really I would. But we're a little overstretched just now. We've got the leadership elections coming up next month, remember. Six different tendencies are putting up candidates, and there's one hell of an ideological stushie over the new leaflet against the West Lothian hospital closures. Not to mention next week's subcommittee to debate the resolutions for the Regional AGM. And, with respect, your particular case is a bit dicey right now . . . That whole gay rights thing is still a hot potato. Really blew it for the Left in the old days . . . No offence, mind, but you have to understand it's a real turn-off for ordinary working people . . .'

Dill sees red. And it isn't just his tie, which she would like to fasten somewhat more securely around his windpipe.

'Are you telling me only the middle classes are queer? No gay hospital porters? And all your canteen ladies certified as happily married heterosexuals? All those nurses just waiting for the day when handsome Dr Mills or that smouldering surgeon Mr Boon will sweep them out of the wards and into a suburban dream kitchen of their own?'

'Now be fair, comrade. I'm not prejudiced. I'm a socialist. We're all in this struggle together. What I think you should do is take up the case with the BMA. They're supposed to look after doctors' interests, aren't they?'

'Screw that bunch of pinstriped patriarchs. I've been paying my sub to this union for a dozen years, and I've done my bit for everybody else's rallies and picket lines and strike funds. Now I'd like a little bit back.'

'Sorry, Doctor, no can do. We've got some serious issues on our hands.'

'I feel for you, comrade. The next time you break a leg, just call a meeting . . .'

Dr Dillon is not the only one with troubles. I think there is a convergence in our planets.

I prefer to keep a low profile, but somehow I am noticed. I can't think why. Could it be the exotic smell of my cooking? My unusual style of dress (my trusty old Proto-Pictish homespun cloak over a pair of present-day denim jeans)? Or my convenient method of lulling the twins to sleep: (1) Conjure up one very tall tree. (2) Insert in patch of concrete outside tower block, with branches rising to height of relevant bedroom window. (3) Fill with nightingales and stand well back.

Whatever the cause, someone spills the beans. Two inspectors from the Social Loans Fund Fraud Squad, one male, one female, arrive at my door at 7 a.m. on a Sunday morning. They are ill-tempered after their climb up the nine flights; the lifts are broken again.

The inspectors thrust a piece of paper under my nose and push past me. The woman makes straight for the bedroom, lifting up the sheets in search of bodies, checking under the bed for alien shoes of the opposite gender, shuffling through the scanty contents of the wardrobe. The male inspector heads for the bathroom to count toothbrushes. He returns to the sitting-room to find his partner struggling to keep her balance. My clever twins have wrapped themselves round her legs.

'Come on, missus, tell us what you've done with him.'

I am perplexed.

'He's bound to be here somewhere. Don't tell me he's away out jogging.'

'Who?'

'Your unauthorized cohabitee.'

'My what?'

'The man you live with.'

'There is no man.'

'We have it on good authority. Deep voices heard at all hours. Comings and goings. Wild parties. Sounds of . . . sex.'

'Whoever told you this is dreaming. Or lying. May their teeth fall out before breakfast.'

'You girls are all alike. Trying to deny it. You know the rules, dearie. If someone is screwing you, it's his job to keep you; not ours.'

I look into their empty eyes. The female inspector screams as two identical sets of teeth fasten themselves to corresponding portions of each ankle. 'Call them off!'

'My girls have minds of their own,' I explain, with pardonable pride. However, the offer of a handful of sweets gradually persuades them to turn their attention elsewhere.

'Spoiled brats,' mutters the male. 'Need a father's firm hand, they do.'

'Men do not come here,' I repeat.

The inspector looks at me with renewed interest. 'Are you a lesbian? If so, you don't qualify for Family Assistance Loans.'

I decide to be puzzled. 'Which tribe is this?'

The woman nudges her colleague. 'This is a waste of time. Let's go.'

At the door, she turns and points a finger.

'You just take this as a warning, dear. Keep your nose clean and your bed empty.'

They depart. I do not bestir myself to transmute them into vermin, or wreak any other suitable revenge. The nimble-fingered youths of the scheme have saved me the trouble, as my tormentors will discover when they reach what remains of their car.

The respectable members of Edinburgh's distinguished medical fraternity do many interesting things to pass the time. They appreciate fine wines, patronize the galleries, exchange witticisms at each other's dinner parties, and indulge in hill-walking, squash and other wholesome sports. What they do not do is wrap abusive messages round rocks and throw them through the handsome astragal windows of the corporate headquarters of Scothealth plc in Heriot Row, and the hideous plate-glass façade of Adam Smith Mutual, in a less fashionable district of the town.

For this reason the police force is surprised, and somewhat titillated, when it apprehends Dr Dillon in the second of these operations. To make matters even more peculiar, she does not even have the classic professional excuse of being a smidgin tipsy after a little too much claret at the Surgeons' Hall. She is stone cold sober, although smiling, when they take her to the cells.

*

I, meanwhile, am undergoing my own initiation into the ritual mysteries of late Hanoverian officialdom. On the day that Dr Dillon is being photographed and fingerprinted, I am sitting on an orange plastic chair in the waiting-room of the Housing Repairs Appeals Tribunal. Forty or fifty people are ahead of me in the queue. The twins grow restless; I resort to my usual trick of hypnotizing them with a twitch of my little finger, and wonder if the same treatment might be applied with good effect to the other infants swarming about the premises. It has taken me three days to arrange this appointment; there seem to be places where the writ of ancient magic does not run. (No telephone inquiries. Personal callers only. Bring all appropriate documents. No incomplete applications will be considered.) I have been warned by the woman behind the glass partition that the day and time marked on my card are only approximate, and I would be well advised to make no arrangements for the rest of the working week.

I have forgotten to bring anything to read (getting the twinlets fed, dressed and organized for the outing took all my concentration). Nor can I forget my dignity enough to plug a little noise-box into my ear and bounce to its secret music. Others around me have no such inhibitions. I don't bother to engage my neighbours in conversation – a waste of time, when I can read their thoughts. One by one, at long intervals, they disappear behind the screens.

And so the day passes. The twins consume three boxes of alphabet biscuits, half a dozen bags of chocolate buttons and the same quantity of potato crisps before my number is finally called. The woman in the glass cage, jabbing savagely at a keyboard and peering at a greenish screen, points to a corridor, where another stern-faced priestess waits. Shielding herself behind a clipboard, she ushers me into a room with no windows.

'Listen for your number. And keep those children quiet, please!'

In the distance, a male voice calls out my number. I negotiate the pushchair back into the empty hallway, see only closed doors, and wonder what to do.

'Get a move on!'

I track the voice to its source, at the far end of the corridor . . .

'Put those children somewhere else!' A secretary springs to attention, and wheels off the twins to points unknown.

'Sit down.'

I am directed to a high stool, facing a long table where three dark-suited officials loll on padded leather thrones.

'You're the lady complaining about the fungus on her walls. Correct?'

I nod.

'What's the matter with it?'

'It is slippery, bright green, and growing every day.'

'Speak up, can't you? Damned funny accent. I thought we'd repatriated all the immigrants.'

I repeat the statement.

Someone chortles.

'Clashes with the William Morris wallpaper, does it?' Collective guffaws by admiring colleagues. The speaker winks at them and turns to me again. 'Now, dear, it's a perfectly natural substance, you know, nothing to be afraid of. It's caused by . . . climatic conditions. Condensation. Moisture in the air.' He glares at me accusingly. 'Do you go in for a lot of nookie?'

'What?'

'You know – heavy breathing. With your old man.'

'There is no man.'

'Well, what about those bairns? Bathe them often, do we?'

'Every day. Like the book says.' Ever the scholar, I have obtained a handbook to guide me through the mysteries of modern mothercraft.

'Well, what do you expect, then, when you're making all that steam. You should open a window, madam.'

'This would make the children cold.'

'Rubbish. At my school we had to run naked down an unheated stone passage to the showers. Did us a power of good!' He thumps his chest.

'The windows are sealed shut.'

'Oh yes, forgot about that. Safety measures in the tower blocks. Can't have the brats defenestrating themselves. Messes up the pavement. Never mind. Now, I see by your file that you have already submitted your complaint three times to the appropriate department. In all three instances, your request has been turned down. Doesn't anything satisfy you people?'

'The house smells foul. Like a cave. The fungus stains our clothing.'

'Well, what do you expect us to do about it? Rebuild your blasted tower? We're not made of money here, you know. And, speaking of money, you are aware that if we do grant your application, the repairs will be charged on the usual scale, plus materials, labour and administrative costs. We could be talking about a rather substantial sum, considering the state you've let the place get into. We aren't a charity, remember. We have to show a profit, same as any other landlord.'

A gentler voice interrupts. 'Are you sure you couldn't simply – learn to live with it? People do like to have plants in their houses. They even go out and buy them at great expense. And here we are, allowing you to enjoy a rather colourful and exotic specimen in your own home, free of charge.'

'Look!'

Time for a little demonstration. I reach into my carrier bag and pull out a plastic box, printed with the name of a local ice-cream parlour. I place it on the table and lift the lid to reveal a bright-green jelly. It trembles slightly as a bubble rises and breaks on its surface, emitting a sulphurous smell.

'This is it,' I tell them.

The officials recoil, but not soon enough. I speak a word and the fungus rises, resolving itself into two small snakes. They glide out of the box and slither across the table. My interrogators sit transfixed.

I look to the man in the middle. He has more chins than the rest. Presumably, the boss. 'Well?'

He gropes for a buzzer beneath the table. Alarm bells sound in the corridor. He splutters into a little box.

'Get the security guards! And the police!'

But help does not arrive in time. When it does, the three officials have vanished. So have their offices. In their place, a gaggle of clerks, receptionists and tenants wander bemused through a flower-dappled meadow, and the only trace of the Tribunal are three empty padded leather armchairs and several hundred floppy disks wafting upwards on the breeze.

*

They catch up with me before the day is out, of course. I am untroubled. Things are now proceeding according to plan.

Behind one of the finest fanlights in Edinburgh's New Town, in a bow-fronted dining-room of perfect Georgian proportions, Lord Corbiestane, High Court Judge, guillotines his breakfast egg. Despite the glory of the summer morning – light flooding through the astragal windows to form a golden gridwork on the tablecloth, birds singing Mozart in the Gardens across the way – he is not in sunny temper.

His sleep has been disturbed by the call of Duty. At some hour after midnight, an urgent appeal from the Colonial Governor extracted him from a saucy dream to sign an Injunction. The large blank patches on the front pages of both the *Scotsman* and the *Glasgow Herald* reveal that the summons came just in the nick of time. One more uncomfortable State Secret is, for the moment, safe.

Perturbed by the possible effects the broken night might have on his golf swing, he taps his spoon upon the sugar bowl. Lady Corbiestane springs up, leaving her toast half-buttered, and carries away the porcelain coffee pot for a refill. As she shuts the door quietly behind her, Lord Corbiestane rummages through the pile of newspapers (he subscribes to all, to keep himself well informed). He extracts an English tabloid, flips it open to the desired page with practised hand, and scowls his disappointment: yet again, the photographer has paid too much attention to bosom, too little to bottom. He wishes someone would write in and complain.

He is deep in the *Financial Times* when the coffee arrives, muttering over the misbehaviour of a stock he would never have touched had it not been for the encouragement of a brother-in-law. He glowers down the expanse of starched linen at the culprit's sister.

'This coffee tastes like gnat's piss,' he announces.

It is not going to be a good day in court.

*

It strikes Dill, on the way to court, that she is the only prisoner in the police van without a tattoo. The two young women sitting opposite, and discussing an interesting professional trick they do with ice cubes, both have skirts slit thigh high: one is marked with a lotus, the other with a rose. Next to them a woman buries her face in hands incised with the letters L-O-V-E and H-A-T-E. And on Dill's left, a wild-haired woman smiles at her with lips adorned with whorls of indigo. Guess who.

Dill thinks to herself, Why only women?

'Ladies' Day,' I tell her.

She jumps. She hasn't spoken.

Silly of me.

The van slams to a stop, and Dill comes flying into my lap. A policeman unbolts the doors, and leers at us.

'Now, girls, none of that, mind, or His Lordship will slap on another month for bad behaviour.'

Lord Corbiestane has an aversion to peculiar women. To his infinite regret, the Public Flogging of Offenders Bill is still wending its way through the pipeline: he would like to see today's parade of female miscreants lashed through the town at the cart's tail, in time-honoured fashion, or well soaked in Dunsapie Loch upon a ducking stool. There was a time when such petty offenders were dealt with in the lower courts, and sometimes Lord Corbiestane regrets the passing of those days. But legal reforms – which he himself helped to draft – have brought crimes against property and offences against Received Morality into the High Courts, to be dealt with by solemn, bewigged senior judges and punished with the same severity accorded to murder, kidnapping and treason.

But economic pressures have changed the face of punishment. Custodial sentences, alas, are out of the question: every cell in Scotland is quadruple-booked. Lord Corbiestane is confident that the situation will, eventually, improve. He hopes that Penal Services plc – in which he is a major shareholder – will soon get its act together, after resisting the hostile takeover bid from Human Reprogramming International, and build the new prisons that were so fulsomely described in its Annual Report.

He opts, perforce, for stiff doses of Electronically Supervised Community Service. Monitoring devices make it possible for prisoners to return each night to their own homes, saving the government a substantial sum on their keep. But no criminal should think that this sentence is any picnic, and so he tells the unsavoury lot who have come before him this morning.

With the efficiency that is the envy of his colleagues, he dispatches the full complement of villainesses well before noon. The only one not given short shrift is the disgraceful Dr Marion Dillon, who is subjected to a brief lecture after sentence is passed. She has, after all, brought discredit upon the entire medical fraternity by stooping to the level of a common hooligan. In the Royal College of Physicians they are beating their breasts, and a gnashing of teeth comes from the Surgeons' Hall; from the spacious bungalows of the Braid Hills unto the stone-built villas of Ravelston and Murrayfield, the professional classes hang their heads in shame.

Enfolded in the majesty of law, His Lordship departs from the courtroom, secure in the knowledge that Queen and Country have been served. He consults his grandfather's gold watch: he should be in plenty of time for the Archdruid's Invitational Lunch at the Lodge. The police van, with its cargo of convicted wrongdoers, heads off in the opposite direction.

As a recent recipient, I can't say I am impressed with this era's version of justice. Where were the hot irons, the haruspices, the observers of bird flight, wind changes and the facial tics of the accused? And I found the sentence downright amusing. Much more so than being roasted alive in a wicker basket during the harvest festival.

Our entire vanload of offenders, for the sake of convenience and cost-effectiveness, has been awarded the same punishment: one month of hard labour for the public good. In this particular case, the public good is served by a variety of maintenance and redecoration jobs at a private golf club on the outskirts of the city. The electronic bracelets bonded round our wrists are programmed not to bleep unless we violate our curfews. I croon a few words in the old tongue at mine, ensuring that it doesn't bleep at all.

One could do worse than spend the long hours of summer daylight out in the fresh air, in the company of interesting women. I feel a slight – only very slight – twinge of pity for dear Albanna, who is presently passing the time in the company of civil servants and their political masters.

'The old fossil could be quite a hot little property,' observes the Secretary of State for Style, passing the port decanter at the Working Lunch.

'The PM seems to think so,' mutters the Minister for Patriotism. 'Claims it will make all the difference in those damned opinion polls. If she can't dredge up a brand-new war to save her bacon, I suppose she hopes an ancient warrior will do the trick instead.'

'It wasn't the Boss's bacon I was thinking of.'

'Message understood. Over and out.'

'I still wish it had been King Arthur,' sighs the Secretary. 'But I suppose we shall just have to work with what we've got.'

'Now, are you quite sure you're not Boadicea?'

'Positive.'

'Well, would you object if we perhaps called you Boadicea?'

'Wouldn't you object if I called YOU Boadicea?'

'Don't be difficult, please. I'm a man.'

'Poor you.'

In the silence, the tea-girl giggles. And melts in the resulting ministerial glare. 'Someone here could lose their security clearance.'

It is Day Nine of Project Britannia at a classified location somewhere in the Scottish Borders. The Adam mansion, formerly an MI6 debriefing centre, has been unused for some time: no one from the East has shown much sign of wanting to Cross Over lately.

The Secretary of State for Style is sufficiently exercised to pull out a pale-blue silk handkerchief and mop his brow.

'You see,' he says, motioning for fresh supplies of tea and trying to be very patient, 'we have a little . . . image problem here. We want someone the public will readily recognize . . .'

'My fame has spread to all the tribes. I am the subject of fourteen

41

songs, eleven legends, sixty ghost stories and at least three Pictish jokes. Now with no disrespect to that Boadicea person – who was, after all, a mere backwoodswoman from the southern wilderness – I am not prepared to hide behind her name.'

'People have heard of her . . . and, with all due respect, madam . . .'

'That's your problem, not mine! Ignorant barbarians! I suggest you refresh your collective memories. I made a promise to return, and I have honoured it. So here I am. You might at least display some enthusiasm.'

'Oh, we are certainly enthusiastic, madam,' says the Secretary. 'We simply want to make the most of your . . . reappearance. If the name Boadicea bothers you, perhaps we could compromise. Introduce you as Britannia. You see, Alba – such as it was – is now part of Britain, after all, so it's really nothing more than a sort of modern translation, and . . .'

'If you people had any religious upbringing to speak of, you would know that a name is sacred. You cannot just change it on a whim . . . any more than you can change a person's sex.'

'We-e-ll,' interposes a smooth young Assistant from the Ministry, 'nowadays, you might be interested to know that . . .'

'Shut up, Nigel!' snaps the Secretary. 'No red herrings wanted today, thank you!'

Unabashed, the Assistant surreptitiously signals his superior to join him for a quiet conference at the far end of the oak-panelled library. 'But don't you see, sir, this could be the germ of an idea . . . What's to stop us actually turning her into King Arthur? I understand the PM would have definitely preferred . . .'

The Secretary of State looks at him thoughtfully. 'Might be a little difficult to arrange it. But an interesting concept all the same. Good example of enterprising thinking, my boy. You'll go far.'

Back in the imperial capital, the Cabinet sit around the boat-shaped table while their mistress steers the ship of State, steadfastly ignoring any storm warnings. The Secretary of State for Style has completed his report on the current state of Project Britannia. The PM expresses a desire to see the prodigy for herself.

'Give us another few weeks,' promises the Secretary, 'and we'll have the product properly packaged.'

The meeting between the two great ladies is duly scheduled. As part of the Cabinet's latest cost-cutting exercise, in preparation for its impending privatization, the visit will be combined with the fact-finding mission to Lochgelly.

'Under the circumstances,' ventures the Media Minister, 'I suggest we make our entry into Scotland with as little fanfare as possible.'

'A good idea,' sighs the Colonial Governor, 'given the Scots.'

'I was thinking', retorts his colleague, 'of the need to maintain a low profile on Project Britannia.'

It is agreed that the journey will not be an Official Visit.

The Minister for Education breathes a sigh of relief. No need for him to muster squadrons of brats to line the roadside, waving Union Jacks. They can stay corralled in their classrooms, struggling with the new North British Core Curriculum: Microchip Assembly, Conversational Japanese, and Tourism Studies (Table Service, Bed-making, and Advanced Cream Tea).

The Colonial Governor reports that accommodation may pose problems. The decayed mining districts of West Fife offer few hotels of charm and character, while the more distinguished hostelries of neighbouring Perthshire are fully booked. The season for Corporate Team-Building Weeks, Sales Seminars, and Coach Tours will be at its peak at the date of the projected Cabinet expedition.

'We could, of course, stay in Edinburgh itself,' proposes the Home Secretary, 'and travel out to Lochwhatsit for the afternoon. Some jolly nice little restaurants in Edinburgh . . . I remember once, when . . .'

The Prime Minister glowers. 'This is a fact-finding mission, not Sunday lunch.'

'Edinburgh,' interjects the Colonial Governor, 'is even more problematical. The time allocated for the Scottish trip coincides with the opening of the city's celebrated International Festival, sponsored by a famous American hamburger chain. Japanese opera companies, Italian orchestras, Bulgarian impresarios and the arts editors of the national press will have filled every decent hotel room.'

'I suppose we could stay in Holyrood,' offers the Secretary of State for Style. 'Enjoy a bit of faded grandeur.'

'The Other Lot have booked it that week,' snaps the PM. 'For one of their ghastly Garden Parties.'

'Damn!' mutters the Colonial Governor. 'I'd forgotten all about it. You do realize that if we are all up there that week, we'll simply have to go.'

'Well, it's your territory, my friend. You sort something out for us somewhere. We can't hold up the day's business any longer. Now, let us move on, gentlemen. There are twenty-six hospitals to be closed, and several hundred drums of imported toxic waste to dispose of before we break for tea. But first I'd like you all to turn your attention to our draft White Paper on the Positive Nutritional Benefits of Acid Rain.'

While Albanna is being prepared for the public eye, our little band of reprobates pays its debt to society at the golf club. We clean toilets, paint the bar, spread sinister weedkiller on the greens, and perform other tasks designed to turn us into model citizens. I haven't had so much fun since Albanna and I were captured and held to ransom by our tribal cousins, the Votadini.

Ill-assorted we may be, but adversity engenders a certain *esprit de corps*. Even L-O-V-E & H-A-T-E, who never speaks a word, warms up enough to nod at the rest of us by the end of the second week. Not that we have much time for sociability: we work a fourteen-hour shift, with three twenty-minute breaks, and the uniformed thuglet assigned to guard us discourages idle chatter. He seems to have learned his trade through a careful study of old moving pictures: *I Was a Fugitive from a Chain Gang*; *Escape from Colditz*; and other epics of your recent past.

'That one wants an electric cattle prod for his Christmas,' observes Kerry, one of the young ladies-of-the-evening, as we scrabble for lost golf balls in the rough.

'And I know just where I'd like to give it to him,' says Marie, her friend with the lotus tattoo.

44

'Personally, I'd like to give him a nasty disease,' mutters Dr Dillon, in a shocking violation of her Hippocratic Oath.

'We could arrange that,' Kerry chortles.

But our gift-shopping plans are cut short by the man himself, bellowing for us to cut the cackle and search deeper in the mud.

I find very few golf balls, although I do turn up several coins from the reign of James IV, and an iron casket containing some juicy gossip about the early Stuarts. I leave them where they are, well buried: why should my temporary employers profit from treasure trove and get the glory?

We are fed every day at the taxpayer's expense: out-of-date potato crisps from the Members' Bar and the day's unsold sandwiches are the usual ration. Our overseer takes his own repast in the clubhouse, and locks us up for safekeeping in the windowless van that rounds us up each morning and takes us to our various homes at night. Here snippets of information are exchanged.

Dr Dillon is gradually dissuaded from giving lunch-time lectures on fascism, class struggle and the patriarchy, and is pumped instead, by Kerry and Marie, for medical advice. I listen politely: I could teach her a Celtic trick or two about curing crab lice and herpes, but for now I hold my peace.

The conversation turns to chickenpox and mumps; I let it be known that I too am – well, for all intents and purposes – a parent. Kerry and Marie's children have been taken into custody, for the duration of their sentences; the two women have been through this routine before, and are matter-of-fact about such occupational hazards. When asked if the twins are also in care, I am evasive.

'Staying at a friend's place,' is all I say. Let the archaeologists puzzle it out when they find Lego bricks, Smarties and Postman Pat jigsaws among Albanna's burial goods: at least my girls aren't bored, and they're out of the traffic.

Dill, fascinated by my tattooed lips, steals sideways glances. She is, however, too well brought up to mention them outright (strange how your people draws its healers mainly from the squeamish classes). I know she would like to draw her fingertip along the whorls and interlacings. But not yet.

*

The back wall of one wing of the clubhouse is sorely in need of repainting. The compulsory labour squad is drafted for the job: this will please the penal authorities, since it counts as Vocational Training and attracts a handsome subsidy.

The slave-driver gives us our orders, and leaves us to it. We are surprised to see Ms L-O-V-E & H-A-T-E pick up a paintbrush with considerable enthusiasm. She is no more likely than the rest of us to curry favour, and more indifferent than most to his sinister threats. We soon discover what she is up to. A devastating caricature of our beloved overseer is quickly taking shape on the grimy wall. Encouraged by our enthusiasm, she produces several more, displaying our hero in various obscene or embarrassing positions. But by the time he turns up on one of his surprise inspections, the drawings have been whitewashed over and we are all hard at work.

Dill and I perch at the top of adjacent ladders, scraping away the old paint from the frames of the lavatory windows. The frosted glass panes are partially open for purposes of ventilation, treating us to the sound of gentlemen members relieving themselves after lunch. We do not find this particularly diverting, until we hear two voices in conversation. The nasal whine of the first party rings no bell, but the pear-shaped drawl of our old friend Lord Corbiestane is unmistakeable.

'Still keeping her very much under wraps, old boy . . . But I thought you might like to know . . .'

'As you say, an interesting possibility . . . when the time comes, I might put the idea to the Board . . .'

'We haven't taken anyone else into our confidence . . . outside senior staff in the appropriate ministries, of course. Always work on the Need to Know Principle. I might slip a word to Roddy, though . . .'

'Hmmph . . .'

'You chaps still not forgiven him for that hostile takeover bid?'

'Bygones are never bygones where my share values are concerned. If he ever has the misfortune to wind up in the dock when I'm on the bench, God help him. I'd hang the bugger for an unpaid parking fine.'

'But you might find co-operation on this little wheeze to be to your mutual advantage . . .'

'I'd consider it. We'd have to see the . . . er . . . lady first. Not interested in pigs in pokes. Anyway, how do you know she's not some kind of fraud?'

'Oh, we've had her thoroughly checked out. And the boffins are convinced. They haven't been able to trip her up on anything. Historically, linguistically, archaeologically, what have you.'

'Extraordinary. Ancient British Amazons. Whatever next, I say.'

'Ah well, best be getting back to the others. Must make the most of my day off. It's back down to Whitehall in the morn. Ready for me to beat the trousers off you on the course?'

I look at Dill. She stands frozen, paintbrush in hand, looking thoughtful. We say nothing until after the flush of urinals and the banging of the door.

'That mean anything to you?' I inquire coolly.

'I think they were talking about . . . ah . . . someone I know.'

'The unsavoury Roddy?'

'No.' She looks slightly bemused. 'The . . . um . . . Amazon.'

'Is that so? What a coincidence. You know, I think we may have a friend in common . . .'

'RIGHT, YOU TWO IDLE BITCHES,' comes a roar from the ground. 'SHUT YOUR FACES AND GET THAT SCRAPING DONE, OR YOU'LL BE UP THERE ALL FUCKING NIGHT UNTIL IT'S FINISHED.'

Albanna's arrival has posed a ticklish challenge to your current rulers. They have risen to their present eminence by harking back – in word, if not in deed – to the values and verities of certain earlier ages. If they had been consulted beforehand, they probably would have ordered up someone from a more recent, and more popular, period in history to serve as their all-singing, all-dancing icon of Britain Great Once More. But they weren't (market research is not in my bag of tricks). Nevertheless, they roll up their handsome handmade shirtsleeves and get on with the job. I look forward to seeing what they make of her.

'So, to conclude, we're . . . ah . . . running just a little over budget. But we think the extra time and effort will be money well spent.'

The PM drums impatient fingers on the table. 'And exactly which purse do you intend to draw the excess from?'

'There's still a bit left in the Public Opinion Adjustment kitty,' offers the Media Minister.

'Better leave that where it is,' the Chancellor interposes. 'We'll need it for Phase Two of the Traditional Family Values campaign. Support for the Sexual Normality Bill didn't come cheap, you know.'

'As agreed by the working party,' says the Minister for Patriotism, 'we've put out one or two very discreet feelers. Just among our own most trusted supporters. On the subject of Private Sponsorship.'

The PM beams at him. Such a wise decision to gather him back into the fold after those silly little amorous peccadilloes. 'Can you tell us more?'

'Well, our friends in the Private Health and Pharmaceutical industries are very intrigued. As you'd expect, given the circumstances. They've touched on the possibility of some sort of . . . research facilities . . . only in the long term, of course. After the fuss has died down. And, in the shorter term, we've had considerable enthusiasm from one of our major defence contractors.'

'Defence? Really?'

'They're about to launch a new line of radiation-proof armoured tanks.'

'A long way from the old girl's wicker war chariot, isn't it?' chuckles the Chancellor.

'I think the image they want to project is Durability. British Armaments Last For Ever.'

The PM allows herself a thin smile. 'Well, draw up a list. Let's see how good the offers are. We could be on to a winner. In the meantime, I look forward to our visit to the Debriefing Centre.' She turns to the Secretary of State for Style. 'I hope you're not about to tell me that it will have to be postponed.'

'Well, it might help if we had a few more weeks . . .'

The Scottish Colonial Governor clears his throat. 'With respect, the rest of the northern tour has already been organized. And you've already announced your intention of attending the Holyrood Garden Party. Unless, of course, we want to plan a second trip . . .'

'Absolutely not!' snaps the PM. 'No sense in wasting fuel, now the oil's gone.'

The electronic bracelets, intended to police our movements, are not worth the microchips they run on. So when I am dropped off at the entrance to my tower block at the end of the day's long shift, I disable my tracking device as soon as the van is out of sight. Making a quick detour to recover the twins from their place of safety, I shepherd the girls to the nearest bus stop. We are going to pay a call on Dill.

Fortunately the bus driver does not scrutinize the coins with care: I have given him three old Scots bawbees and a Roman denarius. It is quite sufficient for the run to Morningside.

Without access to my trusty herbal tonics, Dill – like the rest of the chain gang – is worn out after a day under the eye of Scotland's answer to Simon Legree. She sits on the floor, staring dully at the television screen, with a plate of uneaten toast balanced on her knee. It takes her a long time to answer the doorbell.

'A little something for your supper,' I say, offering her a tin of smoked oysters and a jar of Russian caviar. 'Packed with protein to restore your energy.'

She stares, perplexed, at the food, at the twins – and at me.

'They fell off the back of a lorry. The twins and I came by bus.'

'What about the curfew?' she asks, with a nod towards my bracelet.

'Silly thing broke somehow. Never bleeps no matter where I go or how late I stay there. Just hums away as if everything were as it should be. They'll never know.'

She looks tired, but interested.

'If you like, I can do the same for yours.'

I am – no surprises here – invited in. Fresh toast is made and buttered, in honour of the fish eggs. The twins, responding to a particularly potent Pictish lullaby, fall instantly asleep on the sofa.

'I might have a bottle of white wine left somewhere,' she says. 'From the palmy days when I had a pay packet. But it won't be cold.'

'We'll cope,' I reassure her.

She forages. When poured, the wine is cool as the water from a Highland burn. A wasted effort on my part. She hardly notices. Has other things on her mind.

'About this afternoon . . .'

'Our interrupted conversation.'

'I swear that bastard has radar. I thought he was well away across the course, watching Kerry and Marie dig a ditch. Anyway . . .' She is suddenly lost for words. I suppose it's up to me, as usual. But that's what I came for, isn't it?

'We had just discovered . . . a friend in common.'

'Well, not quite a friend, really, but . . .'

Well-trained daughter of the middle rank. Not presuming above her station.

'Very prudent. She abhors overfamiliarity. Can't help it. Brought up in a veritable tangle of taboos.'

'You seem to know a lot about her.'

'I ought to.'

She chews on this, along with her toast.

'We – met. She was here, for a little while. Told us a few things about herself. Asked a lot of questions.'

'Dear Albanna. I wonder if she bothered to listen to the answers.'

Dill looks me up and down. Turns pale under that ruddy out-in-all-weathers Compulsory Community Service suntan. 'You're the . . . ah . . . magician, aren't you?'

'Gwhyldis.'

'She . . . ah . . . mentioned you.'

'I'll bet she did.'

'Not exactly unqualified praise.'

'All bluff. She'd be lost without me.'

'Well, actually she is. Lost. Vanished without a trace. Just wandered off . . .'

'Don't worry. She's doing fine.'

'Do you know where she is?'

'More or less.'

'I don't understand anything any more. Who are you people?'

This could be a long night.

*

But we are barely into the customs, religion and technology (you'd call it magic) of the Crypto-Celtic tribes when the telephone rings.

'I know who that will be,' I say.

'She doesn't have my number.'

'That lady has everybody's number, dearie. That's how she kept her crown.'

I refrain from a smug smile when a regal voice rings out from the receiver. Whatever she has learned about its practicalities, Albanna has still not quite grasped the theory of the instrument. I can hear her clear across the room.

'At last,' announces the mother of my people, 'I am receiving the honours due to me.'

'Where are you?'

'Somewhere beyond the blue hills. In a very comfortable palace. I am not sure of the precise location. We came here in a sealed vehicle. But I think, from the position of the stars, that I am south of you.'

'Who's with you?'

'Some sort of important chieftain. A pretty, blond-haired barbarian, thinks he has a commanding manner – but I could teach him a thing or two. And a retinue of servants – writing, writing all the time, and capturing my voice in little boxes. They are preparing a great celebration. To mark my triumphal return.'

'I was worried.'

'No need. They are most attentive. My every desire is fulfilled as soon as I utter it – well, almost. I sleep in the most luxurious of chambers, dine on the finest viands. I have at my command several perfectly trained slaves, who scarcely leave my side for an instant.'

Dill doesn't seem to like what she hears. 'Are these – slaves – there with you now?'

'Not at this precise moment. As soon as I picked up this instrument, and began pressing the little buttons, the slave on duty went scuttling out of the room. Ahh, never mind, here she is now, and she's brought the blond chieftain back with her – you should see the magnificence of his sleeping robes . . .'

But we are denied the pleasure of further details. The phone, as you will have guessed, goes dead.

*

No, there is no seduction scene that night. What do you expect at the end of an eighty-four-hour working week, even if we do get Sundays off? And what makes you think I am susceptible to the lady's charms?

For the rest of our Community Service stint we have little time by ourselves, but we do exchange occasional nods and glances. It is understood that we will meet again, perhaps in happier circumstances.

CHAPTER THREE

OUR SENTENCES ARE finally over. There is no graduation ceremony when our electronic handcuffs are unlocked, save a snide wink from the boss-man and a cheery 'Be seein' youse aga n!' I will amuse myself, as the nights draw in, by knitting him a sweet little comeuppance.

The legal ramifications of the government's latest round of Moral Standards legislation have heaped fresh burdens upon Lord Corbiestane. Long gone are the summers when he could look forward to the cultural and social delights of Edinburgh's famed Big Mac International Festival: private receptions amid the splendours of the Signet Library, when the local elite meet artistes of world renown; complimentary seats at operas and other gala events for which no tickets can be had for love or money; tables miraculously available in fully booked four-star restaurants; condescending visits to those hot-tipped Fringe Shows destined for greatness in London or New York.

Now, alas, all these pleasures – and the golf rounds necessary to sustain life and useful friendships – must be postponed to another day. His Lordship is barely out of his wig from one day's end to the next. Every seedy little theatre company demands its day in court, to appeal against the banning of its cheapjack cavalcade of sexual and political perversion. Every self-styled pop concert promoter wants to challenge the injunctions upon certain singers and certain songs. Every foppish art gallery owner musters his lawyers to demand the release of certain ill-conceived and allegedly revolutionary artworks, which the State, in its forbearance, has merely confiscated, instead of consigning them to the bonfire they so richly deserve.

Lord Corbiestane gives them all short shrift – the government need have no qualms as to his soundness. But the due process of law still takes far too much time – and the ever-proliferating criminal classes will insist on cluttering up the calendar with their dreary little rapes and murders. Have these people no respect for culture?

This year, preparations for the famous Edinburgh Festival do not impinge much on Dill's consciousness. She is too busy trying to figure out where her next mortgage payment is coming from, and catching up on all that has happened while her back was turned. Shona turns up on Dill's first full day of freedom, full of news.

Bookshops close, publishers (and pubs) shut down; switchboards are silenced, theatres darkened, lives destroyed. Nevertheless, the Sexual Normality Act does not bring unmitigated disaster to all members of the targeted ten (or is it more??) per cent of the population. Some forward-looking entrepreneurs, well attuned to the spirit of the times, prepare to benefit.

One perspicacious entrepreneur sets up an agency called Designer Closets. For a handsome fee, he will provide his clients with the resources they need to protect their livelihoods: a customized heterosexual curriculum vitae, complete with photographs of loving spouse and bouncing babies, plus a complimentary gold wedding band. For an additional charge, he will supply the necessary personnel – for a company dinner-dance, a Rotary Club outing, or a full-scale marriage of convenience. His old friends and new clients are deeply divided: some damn him as a quisling and profiteer; others – the grateful saved – would like to nominate him for the Queen's Award to Industry.

Shona's very much ex-lover Janet is another prudent survivor. She sets up a Sexual Reorientation Consultancy, to train, cajole, or bully clients back into the Straight and Narrow. The project attracts financial backing from many sources, including a Government Enterprise Grant; the only thing it does not attract is customers. But it's early days yet, says Janet, scanning the criminal court reports with a practised eye.

Our Beloved Leader's much-vaunted Return to Victorian Values takes many interesting forms. Peaky-faced Oliver Twists in old scuffed trainers are rounded up for the Compulsory Youth Training Schemes, to patch up crumbling sewer mains or help build the new Tartanland plc All-Weather Leisure Complex in the middle of Glencoe. Tall silk hats are back in fashion for newspaper magnates and major shareholders. Live-in servants once more abound, upstairs and down (their share of the household poll tax is automatically stopped from their wages) and no up-to-date Executive Luxury Flatlet is complete without its foldaway maid's bed in the airing cupboard. And cholera is coming back.

The PM needs little sleep, and never dreams. After dealing with the dispatch boxes, in the small hours, she sometimes roams the capital. In her desk drawer, laid out like entomological specimens, lie the keys to all the public places in the city: some were presented to her, with pomp and ceremony; others have been procured, *sub rosa*, by her undercover agencies.

One favourite destination is the wax museum. Here she lectures Elizabeth I on her errors in Ireland, commiserates with Victoria over the Empire's demise, and exchanges glances with her Prime Ministerial predecessors. She observes her own glossy replica with a critical eye, and makes a note to have the hairstyle updated. On this particular visit she heads straight for the display of Ancient Britons, and is disappointed to find them small, dark and hairy. They are also male, except for one shawled figure bent over a cooking pot. The PM sniffs the air; there is a faint odour of hot mutton fat. She does not linger. She directs her steps towards the Chamber of Horrors, where she refreshes herself with an examination of the rack, the thumbscrews and the Iron Maiden. The tableau of the execution of Mary Queen of Scots never fails to entertain her, but this evening her pleasure is marred: some wag has replaced Mary's severed head with her own.

Back in Edinburgh, Mr Melville is still smarting, metaphorically, over the affront to his dignity on Arthur's Seat. Unable to exact revenge on the mysterious wielder of the spear that pierced him, he turns his attentions to those who witnessed his humiliation. Encouraged by his brethren of the Druidical Lodge, he launches a campaign against the revival of witchcraft in our own time, as exemplified by feminist Goddess-worshippers and other dubious dabblers in hypothetical old religions. The Druids, of course, as responsible members of the community, are eager to point out the differences between these Satanic cults and their own civic-minded fraternity. Letters are written to the quality newspapers, undated shock-horror stories inserted in the tabloid press, receptive preachers encouraged to fulminate in Sabbath sermons. And, as the new school term begins, teachers are warned to exercise caution over arts and crafts projects and classroom window-decorations, in the run-up to Halloween.

Dill and I have made a date. You didn't think I was going to let her slip away, did you? Three days after our liberation from servitude, I turn up in Morningside, as agreed.

'Where are the twins?'

'With Kerry.'

'From the chain gang?'

'She lives in the tower next to mine. We wave to each other from our windows. I gave her a charm against the Unspeakable Itch, and now she can't do enough for me. Her children own a most remarkable collection of small idols. Some that cry, another that speaks when hidden buttons are pressed, one that urinates if turned upside down. And animals! A duck in a blue jacket, a mouse in red breeks, a flop-eared dog with a world-weary, extraordinary smile. I cannot imagine what gods they represent, but the children are permitted to play with them at will. I'm sure the girls will have a lovely time.'

She tries hard to conceal her relief.

'How long is she keeping them?'

'Until tomorrow. Let's run away together.'

Dill looks interested.

'For weeks', I say, 'I've been desperate for . . .'

She looks even more intrigued.

'. . . a sight of the sea.'

(Ha, fooled you. Is that a shadow of disappointment?)

She snaps back. Metaphorically puts her white coat on, goes all brisk and doctor-ish. 'Edinburgh's on the sea. Or the Firth, anyway. You can take the bus to Portobello any time you like.'

I choose to ignore this. 'You have a car, don't you?' Silly question. What doctor doesn't? They do themselves very well, these modern-day magicians.

She looks surprised. Did she expect I was going to carry her off by teleportation?

'An old banger. I'm about to sell it. For scrap, if necessary. Can't afford to keep it any more. I'm not sure it even goes.'

It goes all right. I make sure of that.

'Where are we off to?'

'I'll direct you.'

'Really?'

I give her a look. 'I still know my way around. They haven't demolished the Pictland Hills or shifted the Firth of Forth – so far.'

We head out along the coast road, into East Lothian. Past Musselburgh, where you can no longer eat the mussels – a pity, they used to be delicious. Past the massive hulk that Dill calls a Power Station – funny, that's what we used to call the stone circle at Cairnpapple Hill. Past the beaches peppered with coal dust from the underwater seams. Past the dunes covered with marram grass, following the line of ridges and low hills on the other side of the estuary. Until I tell her to turn inland, taking a narrow road that rises into the Lammermuirs.

'I still have a lot of questions I'd like to ask you,' she says.

'There'll be time.' But not today.

The road degenerates into a track. A helicopter sputters overhead.

Dill bangs on the brakes. 'I don't know where you're taking us, but I think we'd better find another route. That's a police roadblock up ahead.'

'Just keep going.'

'You're joking.'

'I'm not. They won't see us.'

'Be serious.'

'I always am.' And I'm right, too. They don't. We sail past – to the extent Dill's wheezing wreck of a car can sail – unhindered.

'Would you like to explain that?'

'There is no scientific explanation, Dr Dillon. Be glad the warriors in blue didn't ask you for an explanation of your own. Like what we're doing here.'

'Where are we?'

'A highly sensitive classified location. Government property. Unmarked on any recent map.'

We emerge from the wooded track and find ourselves at the top of a low hill, overlooking a bowl-shaped valley. At its centre, surrounded by groves and gardens, sits a large stone house of elegant proportions.

'The nerve centre', I announce, 'of the top-secret Project Britannia. Where our royal friend is being groomed for stardom.'

'I might have known we'd wind up somewhere like this,' she mutters. And does not look pleased.

Ah to be a fly on the wall in an age when aerosol insecticides are banned and fly-swatters out of fashion! Inside the handsome house, an interesting interview is under way.

'It's just as well you've come, ma'am,' purrs the Minister for Patriotism. 'The lady has become somewhat less co-operative. She says she is tired of dealing with minions.'

'We'll see about that,' says the PM in a voice as chilly as the flagstones underfoot. Squaring her shoulders, she flings open the double doors to the library, and finds no one there.

'Well?'

'In her room, ma'am. She asked to be informed of your arrival.'

'So what are we waiting for?'

The PM paces, with the Secretary of State for Style and the

Minister dogging her heels. She is uninterested in the fine view of the grounds, as seen from the library windows, and equally indifferent to the collection of leather-bound rarities that line the shelves. Averting her eyes from the camel-faced family portraits that seem to gaze upon her with disdain, she clears her throat and addresses the Secretary of State for Style, enunciating every syllable with adamantine clarity.

'I hardly need to remind you, of all people, that we are on a very, very tight schedule. I am not prepared to waste the afternoon. Go-upstairs-now-and-get-her-down-here-or-I-want-your-resignation-on-my-desk-Monday-morning.'

But he is spared the necessity. Into the library comes the Debriefing Centre's tea-girl, bedecked in a bright scarlet headband. Her face is decorated, in what appears to be lipstick, with curious symbols. She holds up a small dinner-gong, bangs it three times, grins at the Prime Minster.

'What in God's name is that?' demands the PM, through tightly clenched teeth.

'I think it's the tea-girl,' says the Minister. 'Or, rather, our former tea-girl. As of this minute, she has been given notice. I'll see that she's escorted off the premises ... Now, look here, young woman ...'

But the tea-girl bangs her gong more furiously, drowning him out.

'Right, youse,' she commands, in dulcet Glaswegian tones. 'All three. On your knees for the High Queen. Now!' And collapses into a fit of giggles.

'Don't be ridiculous!' The Minister explodes.

The tea-girl shrugs, turns, goes out of the door, and returns a moment later.

'She says she's no coming in, then.' Sticking out her tongue, the emissary scuttles away.

'Get that woman in here!' thunders the PM. 'By force, if necessary.'

'I'll buzz Security. I might need help. The old girl's remarkably fit ...'

But he is thrown off balance as the door swings open behind him. Albanna, bearing a dustbin lid shield and brandishing a window pole, stands foursquare on the threshold. Her eyes glitter through bars of red and black battle paint as she examines the Prime Minister.

'This is . . . her?' She turns to the Secretary, demanding an explanation. 'That's no queen.'

He launches, not for the first time, into a painstaking explanation of the difference between the Crown and the government. Albanna is not convinced.

'Bring me the real Queen, then. The one who runs things.'

The Minister for Patriotism gravely indicates the PM again. Albanna resumes her inspection, stepping forward for a closer look. The PM backs off a little, unwilling to expose the achievements of her make-up artists to such intimate, unfriendly scrutiny.

'Not terribly impressive,' confides Albanna to her mentors. 'But I shall take your word for it. Appearances can deceive. I once knew a chieftain who rewarded a sorceress for turning him into a toad: he admitted it was a vast improvement.'

She inclines her head, with gracious condescension, towards the Prime Minister as one potentate to another, then launches into one of her ceremonial specials:

> 'Hail, southern chieftainess!
> Albanna, daughter of the fire-eyed Brychta,
> daughter of mountain-roaring Wylda,
> daughter of sea-watching Hrnwy and,
> unto the eleventh generation,
> daughter of the Dragonspawn,
> Albanna, Guardian of the Haunted Hills,
> Protectress of the Silver Shore,
> Gelder of the Pillage-Men,
> Bids You Welcome!!
> I will tell you of my greatness,
> Oh ye incomers of little memory . . .'

The PM opens her mouth to speak. Albanna ignores her and continues her blank-verse catalogue of victories and shrewd career moves.

Never one to waste a golden moment, the PM signals one of her minions to switch on the tape-recorder: some of this might come in handy for her next address to the Party Conference.

Finally the great Queen stops to catch her breath. The PM grasps her moment, and jumps into the breach: 'Charmed, I'm sure.'

Albanna looks expectant. 'Well, who are you, then? Give us your pedigree.'

The PM smiles. 'I hardly like to bore you with trivial details. I have risen, by my own efforts and initiative, from humble Anglo-Saxon antecedents.' She knows how to play to the gallery, senses this is not enough. 'But who am I, then? Hark!'

She clears her throat, warms to her theme:

> 'Daughter of Thrift and Decency,
> Champion of the Law-Abiding,
> Defender of the Western Empire,
> Scourge of Layabouts,
> Victor of the Southern Sea-War,
> Protector of the Ordinary Family,
> Nemesis of Deviants,
> Spur of Self-Reliance,
> I – am – Mother – England!'

The Minister and the Secretary exchange glances; their mistress never ceases to surprise them.

Albanna is satisfied. She casts aside her improvised spear and shield, sending them rattling and bouncing along the parquet floor, and advances – arms outstretched – towards the PM.

'I think we can do business together,' Albanna announces, with a glittering display of teeth.

That's my girl. As she herself so often reminds me, if you want to breach an enemy's defences, forget the catapults. Charm is cheaper, and much more fun.

'Right,' I say to Dill. 'We can go now.'

She turns the car and brings us back to the main road in a perceptibly frosty silence.

'Any other little surprises?' she inquires.

'Aside from the fact that you have once more passed, unnoticed and unscathed, through an advanced electronic surveillance system and a common-or-garden-variety police roadblock, no.'

A dignified silence is maintained until we reach the car park at Gullane sands.

'I'm supposed to keep an eye on her,' I say. 'That's why I'm here.'

'Thanks for the fulsome explanation. Well, here's your sea. I'm afraid you'll have to share it with a lot of mundane, unmagical picnickers and swimmers. Did you think it would be empty on a sunny summer afternoon? Or are you planning to conjure them all away to make the setting more romantic?'

Damn her insolence. Who does she think she is? I'm the one with the cosmic powers; she's just an anatomical mechanic. I fold my arms across my chest and sulk.

'Maybe two thousand years ago, or whenever, the love scene in the dunes, played to the rhythm of a pounding surf, wasn't such a cliché. But after long service among the vermouth and double-glazing adverts, the scenario has lost its freshness. Try harder.'

'What makes you think there was going to be a love scene?' I reply. (Take that!)

A genuine Victorian blush suffuses those world-weary late-twentieth-century features. I'll bring your colour up, sister, just you wait.

After a delicious lunch of poached salmon, from the Debriefing Centre's own stretch of river, the two great leading ladies begin to warm to each other. They discover that the burdens and delights of power have not changed all that much since Albanna's day.

'Immigration, you see, poses problems. Fresh blood is all very well among the entrepreneurial and investing classes, but lower down the evolutionary scale . . . oh dear. The danger of our own treasured cultural heritage being, shall we say, diluted . . .'

'Quite. The Romans were bad enough, but the rabble that came in after them would set your teeth on edge . . .' Albanna breaks off, and peers intently into the steely blue eyes of the Prime Minister. 'Come to think of it, you look a bit like a Jute yourself . . .'

The subject is smoothly changed.

'Law and order . . .'

'Oh yes. Absolutely. Justice swiftly done. Unhindered by any namby-pamby sentimentality. We gave our villains short shrift, I tell you – into the water with a stone round the neck at the first sign of trouble. Placated the goddesses of lochs and rivers, fed the fish, and kept the crime rate down.'

'Defence?'

'You can't spend too much money on fortress-building. Bung them high as you can get on a commanding rock, and hang the labour costs, say I. But you need back-up: the goodwill of the deities, plus a lot of rough water and bad weather all around you. All very straightforward. But I must confess, with respect, that I find your strategies mysterious. You send up invisible sentinels to patrol the skies, aim flying metal penises at the homeland of your enemies, and apply all the wonders of your wizardry to sustain eternal vigilance and keep your borders tight. And then you go and dig a great long tunnel under the Channel, so the invaders don't even need to get their coracles wet. Yours is a mysterious tribe indeed.'

I wish all the *tête-à-têtes* in the neighbourhood were going so well. My day with Dill is turning out to be something of a disappointment. As I've told you, even the all-powerful can make mistakes. The weather is perfect, just as planned, but, as a point of pride, I am damned if I am going to magic away the people on the beach and give her the satisfaction of being right about my intentions.

We drive back towards Edinburgh. Heading into the afternoon sun, I am dazzled. Something I see, or think I see, by the side of the road makes me cry out: 'Look! Raiders!! Sacking a settlement . . .! Stop the car – we may be able to help.'

'Help who?' asks Dill, slowing down. 'The sackers or the victims?'

'What kind of barbarian do you think I am?'

'In this case, I think the victims of the raid are perfectly happy with things as they are. Perhaps you'd like to have a look.'

We drive along the road for some distance before we can find a place to pull over: the verge is lined with cars and vans.

'Not exactly a surprise attack, you see.'

'What is it?'

'One of the wonders of civilization. A legendary local scrapyard. Whatever you seek shall be found here – broken, bent or painted a disgusting shade of puce, but yours for the taking, at a price. I know people who have furnished their entire houses here.'

We enter the gates, passing a stream of customers carrying off their prizes in the opposite direction; I nearly collide with an excited treasure-hunter bearing a broken cistern on his back. We drift through dangerously tilting wooden huts of mouse-chewed magazines, corrugated iron sheds where the filing cabinets and office desks of a thousand defunct businesses are ranked in wooden and gunmetal rows, with drawers still labelled: Pending, Accounts Receivable, New Products, Carbon Paper, Sales Dockets, Customer Complaints. Cupboards still bear little brown flecks of blood from file clerks' paper cuts; desktops are ringed with the marks of bored tea-drinkers. I can hear scratching pens, jingling bells, and the massed hammering of women's hands on the keys of big black tyepwriters.

'Real dinosaurs, those,' says Dill.

A ramp leads up into a large lorry, minus its wheelbase, where mattresses are stacked in fusty, slithering heaps. We don't linger long, head instead for the objects that seem to be growing in the tall grasses. A cast-iron bath, with lion-clawed feet, contains a load of rusting batteries and fuses. A wooden lectern stands before a matching, high-backed Gothic seat: some previous occupant – a religious or scholastic dignitary, no doubt, from the set of his chin – still sits in it, but Dill does not see him, and I hesitate to draw him to her attention.

I follow her into an old farm building, a byre stocked with books, crammed into tea chests, wooden crates and disintegrating cardboard boxes – old encyclopaedias missing half their volumes, schoolbooks, picture romances, nameless novels by unknown authors, street plans of towns in Belgium, innumerable murder mysteries, hotel guides twelve years out of date. We could be here for hours; I have found the lady's weakness. Perhaps she'd look more favourably on my suit if I helped her turn up a first edition of Gray's *Anatomy*, or an ancient herbal.

'I don't believe it,' she says, holding out a mildewed paperback. 'This one's mine.'

Your Civil Liberties, it is entitled, *An Activist's Guide*. And the name Marion Dillon, in faded red ink, survives on the flyleaf.

'Did you lose it?'

'Lent it. Same damned thing. I wonder how it got here.'

'A miraculous coincidence. It must be fate. You could have it back.'

'At that price? You must be joking. And to think this place used to be so cheap . . .'

'I could, as you would say, liberate it . . .'

'Forget it. It's completely obsolete.'

'Not even sentimental value?'

'If I don't have a job by the time winter sets in, Gwhyldis, I'll be tearing up my books for fuel.'

'Take the long view. Look to the future. I always do.'

'And look where it got you . . .'

'To you,' I say, 'and that's good enough.'

(There. How's that for an opener, pal? That should give you pause for thought.)

It does. About fifteen seconds. Then she starts laughing.

I refuse to be put off my stroke. I continue.

'I've crossed the ages for you,' I whisper (guaranteed more effective than a shout). 'Swum the rivers of oblivion. Wrenched myself from the grasp of the Goddess of the graves. Searched for you in this stone-cold city through a dozen centuries.'

'Don't give us your patter. You're here to take care of Queenie up the road there, that's what. I'm just a chance encounter.'

Charming. We may not have gone a bomb on the old hearts and flowers back in the Iron Age, but at least we appreciated a good line when we saw one.

She puts her hand on my shoulder. I jump: no one's touched me that way in several hundred years. 'Never mind,' she says. 'Let's get back to town. Have you ever tasted Chinese food?'

At the Debriefing Centre, girl talk – Iron-Lady-style – proceeds apace. The PM has just explained to Albanna that it is in her own interest that she be accompanied by minders at all times. Not merely for her own safety in a world full of dangers that – with the greatest respect – may be hard for her to comprehend. Not because her hosts don't trust her. But because All The Best People have them: the attendance of a muscular guard, with low forehead, walkie-talkie, and suspicious bulge under the jacket, is what marks out the movers and shakers from *hoi polloi*.

Albanna understands completely. There have always been little rituals to distinguish Us from Them.

All rulers, she informs the PM, with the condescension of one who has been around a little longer, have been constrained by some form of taboo. Restrictions, she explains, are the lifeblood of monarchy. By way of illustration, she cites certain kings of Pictland: forbidden to speak to any pregnant woman wearing earrings on a Tuesday, or to walk widdershins around a billy goat, or to eat cabbage cut when the moon was new. She herself boasts a long and charming list of bans: wetting her hands after sunset, for instance, which precludes helping with the washing-up, or eating salt in the presence of strangers, which is a good way to turn down unwanted dinner invitations without giving offence.

Even Albanna's brief experience of the current scene convinces her that her contemporary counterparts must have their own collection of taboos. She doubts that any Royal would scratch an armpit in the presence of a camera; nor can she envision the Prime Minister standing in a bus queue in the rain. Presumably, if she dared to do so, the angry gods would send plague and famine long before they sent a Number 7 bus.

'People never appreciate the terrible sacrifices we make on their behalf,' Albanna sighs.

The Prime Minister agrees.

What is this creature trying to do to me? With two little ivory sticks, she presses morsels of inconceivable deliciousness between my lips. Crisp, succulent, pungent, garlic-scented, mellow, fiery, sour, sweet.

Is this a meal or a magic ritual? Perhaps civilization has not gone totally downhill.

She offers me the last amber morsel of crackling duck-skin, as she licks the spicy coating from the carapace of a crab.

As one hunger is sated, another grows more insistent. I am driven mad with lust. Whatever she might think, that wasn't idle patter this afternoon, back there on Gullane beach; I am smitten.

Dill is not receiving, or is deliberately ignoring, my subtle signals. She pours me out another cup of the steaming nectar brewed from Eastern flowers. Chats away about the regional differences in Chinese cuisine. (Where's China, anyway?) Seems quite oblivious. This is unusual for one in my exalted position. Normally, they fling themselves at my feet. Not that I encourage it. I can tell the difference between attraction and ambition.

Perhaps I misread her? I must be out of practice. If I weren't so vain about my own charisma, I'd try a charm. But I want her to want me for my own sweet self. So I don't.

'If you really don't have to get home for the twins,' she says, 'would you like to come back and watch the late movie? Another important cultural artefact. It's *The African Queen*.'

'I thought you'd had your fill of Queens today.'

She suppresses a smile. 'All will be revealed.'

That's better. I knew I hadn't lost my touch.

I am confused. The woman with the remarkable cheekbones is not, it turns out, a Queen at all. And I cannot think what Dill finds so wonderful about the story's ending. A perfectly good boat destroyed. The unshaven man with a voice like a quacking duck is quite irrelevant. Dill defends the story and its stars. Before the argument heats up, she withdraws to the kitchen, then calls me in.

'You're not the only one who can make magic,' she announces. 'Watch this.' She takes a fistful of hard yellow kernels, drops them into a pan with some sizzling oil, bangs the lid on, and holds it down. 'Right,' she says, 'here's the spell.' Shaking the vessel violently, she mutters: 'Key Largo Painted Desert African Queen Treasure-of the Sierra Madre Big Sleep Maltese Falcon To Have and Have Not-Casablanca etcetera. There!' Something is happening within the pan, which now seems to be occupied by a party of small demons, hissing, spitting and battering against the sides.

She lifts the lid. A mountain of white cloudlets spills into a waiting bowl. 'Butter. Salt. Cayenne pepper. Taste it.'

I am dazzled. Have I met my match?

'There's something I think you ought to know,' says Dill, licking the last streaks of butter from her fingers.

'Yes?' Here it comes. The vow of chastity. The absent lover due back in an hour. Some things never alter.

'My bedroom's a mess.'

'That changes everything.'

And I do. It takes only a single word of power. We find ourselves in a moss-lined cave, warmed by a fire of sweet-smelling branches, lulled by the sound of a distant sea. It may not be popcorn, or Szechuan duck, but even she has to admit it's a damned good trick.

What happens next, I am not at liberty to disclose. Especially not under Section 82 of the new Sexual Normality Act. So, for your own protection, do not imagine waterfalls, nightingales, shooting stars, damask roses, or eagles on the wing; ignore all opening buttons, warm skin, moving hands, tongues, lips, fingers, or anywhere they might come to light. Do not believe that anyone was pleased, fulfilled, ecstatic, or otherwise made happy; that fires were lit, bonds forged, loneliness ended or longings answered. Otherwise you run the risk of being recruited, corrupted, polluted, and probably arrested. Take my advice and shut your ears and eyes. Or, better still, close this book, find a socially acceptable spouse of the opposite gender, turn off the lights and assume the missionary position. I would not want anyone prosecuted as an accessory to our crime.

A ringing telephone next to his bed invades the dreams of the Scottish Colonial Governor. Once again, he is sitting an exam he has not prepared for, wearing only a tartan tea towel, while the Prime Minister holds a stopwatch the size of Big Ben. He shakes himself awake, reaches for the receiver, and sees by his digital clock that it is just after 4 a.m.

'Good morning! I trust I am not interrupting your breakfast.' The PM sounds daisy-fresh, as always: her minimal sleep requirements excite the envy of her enemies and the loathing of her subordinates.

'Not at all!' he croaks, then clears his throat. 'Ahem. That's better. Bit of the last croissant slipped down the wrong way.'

By his side, the Colonial Governess moans loudly in her troubled sleep. He claps a pillow over her head. 'Now what can I do for you, on this fine and . . .' He reaches out to open a curtain, cranes his neck, falls out of bed 'Ow! Damn! . . . rainy morning?'

'It's about that wretched Garden Party.'

'Oh, they'll run it all right, rain or no rain. I'm afraid we can't get out of it that easily . . . If you really cannot face it, ma'am, we can cry off by pleading pressing Affairs of State. I could make a few phone calls if you like, cobble up a national crisis of some sort . . .'

'We don't want to get out of it!' comes the reply. 'In fact, we've decided we wouldn't miss it for the world. That's why we're ringing. To ask you to get on to the Holyrood security people and tell them there will be an additional member of the Prime Ministerial party . . .'

'Right you are. Does that mean your good man has decided to forgo the golf at Muirfield and come along?'

'Of course not!' she snaps. 'Think again!'

For a split second, he imagines he is still dreaming. Looks down to check if he's wearing the tea towel. He is not.

'With respect, ma'am, surely you aren't planning to take that . . . hairy-legged Celtic person?'

'Albanna, as you will know if you have perused the briefing paper I sent over at least two hours ago, is a very honoured guest of this government. With particularly strong regional connections which you, in your – ah – delicate political position, should not fail to appreciate. What's more, we've cleaned her up a little. Not without a tussle, I'm afraid. But she'll do well enough for Holyrood. And it will do us no harm to let the story break here first. A bit of a dry run for the real thing, when we take her South at the end of next week. Plenty of photo opportunities, and costs us absolutely nothing. Besides, I can't wait to see the expression on That Woman's face when I introduce her and the rest of her half-German gang to some genuine true-blue British royalty. That should put them in their place.'

All over the Central Belt, from Milngavie to Coaltown of Balgonie, in ancient Royal Burghs and concrete new towns, excited people are looking into mirrors. They struggle with their ties, stroke the flowery silks of summer frocks, check morning coats to see the hire-shop labels are well concealed. Loyally, they ignore the rain – a fine, drenching Scotch mist, transparent as a bridal veil – that hisses down upon their Georgian terraces, double-glazed sub-urban bungalows, crow-stepped manses, ancestral seats with fine green views, bought and not quite paid for ex-council houses on one of the really-very-nice-you'd-never-know-it-was-once-public-sector estates. They suppress worries about getting wet; they are off to bask in the Monarch's sunshine.

Taxis, Daimlers, Land Rovers, company cars and electric wheel-chairs deliver the lucky throng to the palace gates. Necks are craned in search of friends or famous faces. Lord and Lady Corbiestane have come to Holyrood because they are of the class that always does; the *frisson* for them is the loudly proclaimed ho-hummery of it all. They will hardly notice – and certainly not converse with – those fellow-guests who plan to frame their Invitations to hang for ever above the coal-effect gas fire in the lounge. Mr Melville, like a few hundred others, is here in honour of his services to the community: twice a year his Druids send a minibus-load of urban urchins up North to be quick-marched over peat bogs and deposited in the depths of a conifer forest with only a penknife and a bouillon cube, for the purpose of building backbone and developing moral fibre.

Marquees and marked-out pathways corral the sanctified few who have been chosen, after careful vetting, to exchange a word with Them. The rest mill about under their umbrellas, clutching crustless sandwiches, nerving themselves for the scrum at the strawberry tent. Long queues form at the portable lavatories: contact with Royalty stimulates the bladder. When the Royal hat and handbag emerge from a seventeenth-century door, the rain obediently stops.

The Prime Minister rides in at high noon, backed by her pinstriped desperadoes. The crowds part and murmur. Albanna troubles them. Is this an emissary from some exotic ex-colonial realm, just ever so slightly late for the last Royal Wedding? Or could tattoos be a new Garden Party rule, like a hat for Ascot?

The meeting of the three great ladies is an historic encounter, made even more interesting by the fact that two of the trio are discreetly snubbing each other, while the third is giving them both the glad eye in a way that shocks them silly. But the scene, alas, is lost to public view. Each potentate is surrounded by a set of minders far taller and burlier than herself: only a peacock feather on the Prime Ministerial hat bobs up above the melee.

The interview does not last long. The royal equerries take pains to remind their mistress that she has four hundred and seventeen more hands to shake before tea time. It is also marred by a small punch-up between The Royal Company of Archers and the camera-popping tabloid press, who have slinked into this normally forbidden ground at the PM's invitation and nearly succeed in shooting the unfortunate moment when Albanna throws her arms around a startled Queen. A nasty episode is avoided, just in time, when a Royal daughter-in-law heaves into view with a hiked-up hemline and a plunging cleavage: the pack forget their assignment and run baying after her.

'Put down that strawberry and get to a phone,' says the PM to the Colonial Governor through tightly clenched teeth. 'If we lose the headlines, Game-Plan Two goes into action: I want a three-minute spot on the six o'clock news.'

It's a long time since I've felt so cheerful after an all-but-sleepless night.

'Well?' says Dill.

'Well?' I answer.

'Would you like some breakfast?'

'Wasn't that it?'

'Shameless . . . I mean fresh-squeezed orange juice, croissants, my Auntie Jessie's legendary homemade raspberry jam . . .'

'And twins, I'm afraid. I said I'd pick them up before eleven. I can't impose on my babysitter's goodwill for ever. We might need her again some time.'

'Not might. Will.'

'Yes? I'm flattered.'

'I'm serious.'

We draw a veil. The twins can wait a little longer. So can the croissants.

That morning we are not divided. Dill even offers to come with me to collect the twins. Only when I know her better will I realize what an earth-shattering transformation this is.

On our way past a paper shop, with the girls in tow, I suddenly see banner headlines that stop me dead. They are accompanied by several different versions of a very familiar set of tattoos, split by a starry grin.

I leave Dill standing on the pavement, fielding twinly clamours for ice creams and sweeties, rush into the shop and scoop up all the papers. The upmarket ones have front-page photographs of the PM shaking hands with Albanna outside New St Andrews House, a small inset map showing the tribal divisions of Iron Age Scotland, brief statements from the Media Minister: '. . . honoured guest . . . opportunity to learn more about Britain's heritage . . . public appearances in the pipeline . . .'

In the leading bread-and-circuses tabloid, Albanna only makes an inside page, having been upstaged by PRINCESS IN PEEK-A-BOO FROCK SHOCK. The two-paragraph story is headed TATTOOED TARTAN ROYAL TURNS UP, and devotes more space to the other celebrity guests at the Holyrood Garden Party than it does to Albanna. She has made some impression on the journalistic consciousness, however: the large-bosomed maiden whose photograph occupies the other half of the spread carries a spear and a Celtic shield. Apart from a smile, it is the only thing she is wearing.

'You're a fly one,' says Dill. 'I suppose you knew all about this.'

I am mortified. I have been caught out, not paying attention. My invisible antennae otherwise engaged, my scrying crystal fogged by heavy breathing. I can just imagine what Albanna would say to that. I may never live it down.

'I should have. But I didn't. I seem to have had other things on my mind.'

She looks quite pleased with herself. Why shouldn't she? She's not the one with a professional reputation at stake.

'So what do you do now?' she asks.

'I get moving, fast.'

A picture caption in the *Scotsman* indicates that Albanna will be among the guests of honour at tonight's performance of the famous Edinburgh Tattoo. I develop a sudden craving for military pipe bands and motorcycle stunt teams. Dill will be charmed to mind the twins.

CHAPTER FOUR

'FORTRESS OF THE MAIDENS, and hurry, please.'

The taxi driver turns round and gives me a blank look. I remember when I am.

'Sorry. I mean the Castle.'

'You'll be wanting the Tattoo. I hear it's terrible this year.'

We roar off, only to be stopped in Morningside Road by the official Edinburgh International Festival Saturday-night traffic jam. A recital of Burns's erotic poetry, set to Balinese gamelan music, is packing them in at the Church Hill Theatre; further down the road, at the King's, rave reviews of the Vladivostok Mime Ensemble's radical new interpretation of *Mother Goose* have choked the streets of Tollcross with excited culturati. We turn off into the back streets just in time to avoid the riot in snarled-up Lothian Road, where several dozen people in evening dress and an equal number in carefully faded denim are brawling over a parking space equidistant from the Filmhouse, with its Japanese soap opera retrospective, and the Usher Hall, where the annual Symphony Concert of Safe Classics for Rich Corporate Patrons is about to begin.

The driver stops just past the statue of Greyfriars Bobby, invisible within a ring of camera-snapping tourists. They are arguing loudly in several languages about the proper speed of film for a bright summer evening.

'If it's all the same to you, hen,' he says, pointing to the long lines of luxury coaches double-parked as far as the eye can see, 'you'd be as well to walk up to the Tattoo from here. It could take me half an hour just to get you round the corner.'

I wonder if this is a good idea. Maybe it would be better if I appeared to Albanna in her dreams; it's a tricky technique, but I could try it.

But there is no point in hesitating. A chattering, umbrella-poking, tartan-rug-toting crowd of determined Tattoo-goers presses at my back, cutting off any chance of escape.

'Ticket, please, miss.'

Damn. I should have thought of that. There's not a last-minute seat to be had. A look at the customers around me confirms that these are people who Always Plan in Advance. Only one option: I fix the ticket-collector with a haughty stare, one eyebrow raised in a perfect Gothic arch.

'Ah, yes, ma'am. VIP enclosure just along to the right.'

I am greeted with deference; it seems they think I am some form of contemporary pop star. Must be the nifty new face paint. As a nod to the occasion, I have abandoned my usual tribal markings in favour of a little Union Jack on either cheek. Dill says she hates it; I have promised to wash it off as soon as I return. But that will not be for some time yet; it appears that I am going to be stuck here all night.

The VIP seats are, of course, far more comfortable than those assigned to the common herd. They enjoy the finest view, the clearest sightlines, and, unfortunately for me, the best acoustics. Every fanfare twangs in my spine, every drumroll and cannonade rattles my jaws. I am hemmed in by several rows of Distinguished Visitors, and a few well-scrubbed upper-crust children with bell-like voices; perhaps I should have brought the twins for protective camouflage.

Three rows in front of me is a little roped-off enclosure, where the empty seats are even more comfortably padded. Suddenly a little *frisson* of interest ripples through the ranks of advocates, lord provosts, managing directors and colonels' ladies: the Prime Ministerial party has arrived. They are surrounded by blank-faced men staring in every direction at once, murmuring into portable telephones. As well as the PM, the Scottish Colonial Governor, and other members of the Cabinet, the little band includes a number of distinguished hangers-on and political supporters. Necks are craned politely as the people around me whisper the names of a television game-show host, a newspaper mogul, and a champion golfer.

But only one celebrity in this gaggle interests me. And here she comes, flanked by two burly minders of her own. The PM beckons and pats the empty seat beside her. A split second before the Tattoo begins, I open my mouth and give Albanna our usual signal: the mating call of a black-backed gull. My neighbours seem quite startled. Albanna, bless her, looks in every direction but the right one. I draw her attention with an ululation that completely drowns out the opening bars of the Welcoming Fanfare and March, as performed by the Regimental Band of the Countess of Sutherland's Own Displaced Highlanders.

I'm glad to see I still have a little influence. When she finally catches sight of me, not all the Queen's horses, nor all the PM's men, can restrain her. With the agility born of eighty-six successful raids on enemy brochs and duns, Albanna vaults over the astonished heads of the Scottish Establishment. She lands in my lap.

'So there you are. I've been wondering when you'd turn up. You deserve to be throttled.'

I ignore this remark, merely stand up and brush her off my knees like a lapful of crumbs.

'It's time we had a talk,' I say, glowering down at the heap of outraged Queen.

'My hosts will tear you to pieces,' announces Albanna, rising and dusting herself off.

We have completely upstaged the Tattoo, as far as this little patch of audience is concerned. The PM and her minions have turned round in their seats, desperate to see what their guest is up to.

'I hate to tell you, dearie,' I say, 'but your hosts are a pack of rogues and bandits. I'm afraid you've fallen in with bad companions once again.'

Albanna beams at me, and opens her arms. 'Nag, nag, nag. Hello, darling. Nice to see you haven't changed . . .'

We exchange the traditional greeting between sovereign and spiritual adviser. Lady Corbiestane to the left of us, and the Marchioness of Gruinard to our right, instantly faint dead away. Sorry, ladies, that's the way we do things in the Fortress of the Maidens.

'Lots to tell you . . .'

'Likewise,' I reply. 'And this is not the place.' Especially not when

76

I see two government-issue gorillas with conspicuous bulges under their leather jackets standing at either end of the row.

I indicate their presence to Albanna. 'Your hosts are very solicitous. They seem reluctant to leave you to your own devices for an instant.'

'They have been a little overattentive,' Albanna agrees. She waves gaily at the PM, who is now standing with arms akimbo, bellowing for her to return to her place at once. The security men are making their way towards us, edging past our important neighbours with hastily murmured apologies.

I wink at Albanna. She nods at me.

A sudden, unscheduled bang from a cannon dislodges a vast flock of pigeons from the castle ramparts. Their panic-stricken flight releases a deluge of droppings. By the time the two security men have wiped the slime from their eyes, we are somewhere else entirely.

The Prime Minister is too busy to notice, as she struggles to remove a corona of slippery gobbets from her cast-iron coiffure. All around her, Cabinet members dab at their own bespattered pinstripes. Only the Chancellor of the Exchequer remains – miraculously – unmarked. He stares, disbelieving, at the open box of Belgian chocolates on his knee. Ruined, every last one of them – and before even a single fresh-cream truffle has passed his lips.

At the Debriefing Centre, which the Prime Ministerial team has taken over as its base camp, the lights burn through the night. The PM sits in a barber's chair while a team of security-vetted, certified-heterosexual hairdressers extract the bird droppings and repair the Official Hairstyle.

The Secretary of State for Style and the Media Minister bend over a lightbox, checking the comb-out against transparencies of official portraits and newspaper photographs to make sure the reconstructed coiffure is perfect in every detail. Without this vital task to occupy his attention, the Scottish Colonial Governor paces up and down the room, pausing at regular intervals to peer through the windows at the moonlit grounds.

'Would you mind sitting down, sir?' ventures the senior hairdresser. 'Every time you stop at the window, Madam's head turns . . .'

Madam herself is less deferential. 'Stop hanging around that window, for goodness' sake!' she snaps. 'I hardly think the damned woman is about to come up the drive in a taxi. We wish you'd been this vigilant before she bolted.'

The Colonial Governor blinks. This is clearly unjust. He was sitting at the far end of the row when the incident occurred.

His boss, as she so often does, appears to read his thoughts. 'And it's no use your telling me you weren't sitting anywhere near her at the Tattoo. This is your territory, and I expect you to be in charge.'

'Every police officer in Lothian and the Borders has been drafted into the search. Plus a reinforcement of tracker dogs from Strathclyde. We'll run her to ground.'

'Damned shame to waste last night's photo opportunities . . .' sighs the Media Minister. He has a fancy for the Colonial Governor's job. So much handier than Whitehall for the grouse moors.

The PM fixes her gunsights on this new target. 'Well, we'll just have to do our best to salvage something out of this cock-up, won't we? That's what we're paid for.'

The Media Minister bends deeper over his transparencies, wishing he'd kept his mouth shut. He remembers that the Northern Ireland slot is still vacant, after the previous incumbent's nervous collapse.

'Would Madam like to see for herself?' interposes the hairdresser, offering a hand mirror and whirling the PM round in her chair.

She takes the mirror, and propels it across the room. It strikes the Colonial Governor – who is staring out of the window again – squarely between the shoulder blades, then ricochets on to the parquet, where it shatters.

'Seven years' bad luck is only a fleabite compared to what's coming to Scotland, my man, if you don't find that woman by the time our Corporal Punishment working party gets back from the leather strap factory in Lochgelly. It is now 3 a.m. That gives you exactly thirteen hours. If Albanna is not sitting in this room taking afternoon tea when we return, I am fully prepared to telephone our friends in Sydney and Tokyo, and pull the plug on what's left of your industrial base. Then I'll leave you to tell your ungrateful natives the reason why.'

There is an uncomfortable silence. The PM glares from one tightly clenched face to the next.

'Now get out of here, the lot of you. We could all do with a good night's sleep before the morning meeting. You have ninety minutes.'

But the Secretary of State for Style does not choose to spend his free time napping. He slinks along to the suite occupied by the Minister for Patriotism, taps out an agreed-upon signal, and is hastily admitted. The pair withdraw to the bathroom, and turn on all the taps. Their ensuing conversation is obscured by the gushing of water from bath and sink and bidet, but the Minister — aware that one cannot be too careful when it comes to the Debriefing Centre — foils any super-efficient listening devices by flushing the toilet repeatedly as they speak.

'Tears before bedtime, eh?'

'Nothing to laugh about. If the old ghost doesn't turn up, that's our gravy train derailed before it even leaves the station.'

'Not to worry. The local police commissioner's a member of my Lodge. He's given me his druidical word they'll have her back to us by lunch hour.'

'Even so, I don't like the look of it. She's too independent by half. Could be quite a handful.'

'Nonsense. She'll make a perfect figurehead.'

'As long as she knows that's all she is. The lady has some rather antiquated views on power and protocol.'

'Doesn't matter. Once we give the Boss the heave-ho we can buy Queenie off with her own private chef and pastry-cook, and just trot her out for the usual photo opportunities.'

'But how do we broach the subject in the first place?'

'That', smiles the Secretary, 'you may safely leave to me.'

*

While the PM's warriors and their hounds comb the countryside for Albanna, we are only a few steps away from the scene of her disappearance.

'I'm thirsty,' complains the She-Wolf of the North. 'And I haven't had any supper. We were going on to some sort of official dinner afterwards. At an Officers' Mess.'

'Sounds like what happens when you let men run a battle.'

This slips past her; I knew it would. Queens are all alike.

She sniffs the air. 'They're after us.'

Official feet in undercover shoe leather come pounding down the castle hill, and two-way radios crackle.

'In there . . .' We sidestep a green plush turkey on six-foot stilts, handing out leaflets for a late-night Fringe cabaret, and bolt down the mouth of a cobblestoned close. The passage, narrow as a coffin, is a maze of scaffolding, as Mr Melville and his fellow-property developers transform yet another seventeenth-century slum into Elegant Studio Conversions with Period Features. We pick our way down the steep incline towards a doorway, visible under the metal supports, lit by a single bulb. A roughly painted sign announces 'Late Nite Bistro'.

We slip inside, and peer out through a chink in the door to make sure we haven't been followed. Satisfied that the coast is clear (I'm damned if I'll sweat out two teleportations in one night), we find ourselves a table. This is easy: there's only one, and it's empty.

We are in a low, barrel-vaulted chamber, with stone walls oozing the damp of ages and a dusty pair of crimson draperies at one end. Something rustles behind the curtains, and a waiter appears. He is tall, slim, blond, bow-tied and slathered in theatrical make-up. His accent is English and plummy; he could be the nephew or baby brother of the Secretary of State for Style.

He bows, and hands each of us an oversized menu. 'Good evening, and welcome to the Café Listeria, a gastro-improvisational performance event. Are you reviewers? No? What a pity.'

Albanna turns the menu upside down, and studies it. In our day, literacy was not a prerequisite for queenship.

'Would you care for a recitation of our daily specials? There's a warm salad of free-range grey squirrel livers lightly dressed with a hazelnut oil and shallot vinaigrette; a layered terrine of starling breast and wild goose mousse with a coulis of Blairgowrie raspberries; a marinated saddle of . . .'

Albanna stops him. 'None of your frivolous foreign muck for me. I want a slab of smoked pig's belly seethed in grease and clapped between bannocks.'

'Sounds good,' I say. 'I think I'll join you.'

This stops him in his tracks for a moment, but in the end we get our bacon rolls.

We also talk until the middle of the following morning. After some fifteen hundred years apart there is quite a lot of business to sort out, not to mention gossip to catch up on. I also propose to Albanna that we begin to work out our plan of action.

'What plan of action?' she asks.

'Saving your nation, mate. That's what you're here for, remember? Returning to aid your people in their time of distress.'

'Ah, well, yes. Of course.' She muses for a moment, toying with an oversized peppermill, then brightens. 'I am studying the situation. Reviewing the options. One can't just jump in feet first. It all takes time.'

'Just as long as you don't forget why you came.'

She gives me one of her turn-to-stone looks. I am unfazed.

'Listen, spell-spinner, stick to what you're good at. You take care of the mystery and magic. But leave the politics to me.'

'Your hosts seem to be showing you a good time,' I observe, pretending to change the subject.

'I'm to be taken on a tour of the realm, then installed in a comfortable palace somewhere in the present capital.'

'You do know where that is, don't you?'

'South of here.'

'Way, way, way south of here. Many days' journey beyond the borders of the known world. Are you quite sure you want to go?'

'Why shouldn't I? It's the nerve centre of their empire.'

'It's on the banks of that river.'

'What river?'

'THAT river.'

She remembers, looks scandalized. 'THAT river? The one where the flasks are buried?'

'The very one.'

'What a strange place to build a capital. In the middle of nowhere.'

'It was, once. That's why we put the flasks there.'

Albanna has a particular grin that she wears only when she's caught me out. She's wearing it now.

'Now who was it who chose the place to put them? Somewhere inconceivably remote from any of our settlements and sacred sites, I recall you saying. A wilderness of clay flats and forest, completely uninhabited – at least not inhabited by anybody of importance.'

'I hope to goddess they aren't leaking.'

'If I remember our original discussions on the matter – and do correct me if I'm wrong – you claimed you'd devised vessels that were wind- and watertight. That would stay safely sealed for ten times ten generations.'

'Start counting.'

'Hmmh? Ahhh. Oh dear.'

'Of course, there's no way of knowing if the substance is still effective. It could have deteriorated over time.'

'But just to be on the safe side – I remember your exact words – we would send them somewhere far beyond the edge of anywhere for secure disposal.'

'I did try to be responsible in my experiments. Besides, you were the one who was nagging me to distraction to develop a new offensive weapon.'

'I was thinking more along the lines of a fast-acting poison for the enemy's water supply. Anyway, that tribe of scoundrels is not only extinct, but completely forgotten. So it's all water under the bridge by now.'

'An unfortunate analogy,' I say. 'Anyway, if you're determined to go south, better stick to barley-brew and uisge-beatha.'

'They have something better now. It's called champagne. Beats any of your little home-made elixirs into a cocked hat.'

At some point in the small hours I begin to wonder why the waiter shows no impatience, merely reappearing at suitable intervals to bring fresh pots of tea. Albanna, of course, never notices: she expects round-the-clock service as her Goddess-given right.

When I ask for the bill, the riddle is solved.

'On the house, dear ladies,' says the waiter, bowing low. 'Under the circumstances, it is the least we can do. Our budget, alas, doesn't run to Equity rates.'

I look up. The velvet curtains at the end of the room are wide open, revealing not another stone wall but a small auditorium containing three rows of seats. About half of them are occupied. Two or three people snore gently, heads on their chests. A sharply dressed little man scribbles furiously into a spiral notebook balanced on his knee. But the rest of the audience, with circles under its eyes, rises and gives us a standing ovation.

We step out, blinking, into the sunlight. The souvenir shops on the Lawnmarket are already humming with a new day's tourist trade.

A human projectile bursts out from behind a Find Your Family's Tartan poster on the pavement, and executes a flying tackle of Albanna's ankles.

'Gotcha!!'

It is a small, fierce policewoman. She begins to murmur into her radio.

Albanna makes no effort to resist. 'My friends must be eager to reclaim me. How nice to be in such demand.'

She looks down benignly at her captor. 'But you must rise, my dear. I appreciate your deference, but I understand that grovelling minions are out of fashion.'

'I'm not so sure,' I mutter.

Albanna blinks, as if she cannot quite recall where we have met before, then dismisses me with a credible imitation of the Hanoverian royal wave.

'I'm in safe hands now. I'm sure I shall soon be reunited with my hosts. But we must keep in touch.'

Worry not, Queenie. I won't let you out of my second sight.

In the back of the police car, speeding out of town, Albanna seeks to make conversation with the interesting young Amazon who has claimed her.

'Tell me, my dear,' she asks, pointing out of the window, 'what do they call that great hill nowadays?'

'Arthur's Seat, ma'am.'

'WHA-A-A-T?' The outraged roar nearly sends the police driver swerving into the lane of oncoming traffic. 'AARRTHURR'S . . . !!!'

Her escorts look deeply puzzled.

'That upstart! That little Brythonic git! I wouldn't let him put his foot on my territory, let alone plant his fat backside on MY sacred mountain. HIS seat!! That's a good one. Arthur's Seat indeed. I'd like to meet the people who do his PR!!'

'I did say I might be gone for a while.'

Fifteen hours, according to Dill, is not what she understands as a while. I try some mollification.

'For someone who declares herself allergic to small children outside surgery hours, you've coped very well.'

The twins indeed are bright and breezy. They've slept long and deeply – as programmed; I am not that inconsiderate of my babysitters – and seem to have enjoyed their introduction to wholemeal toast, the alphabet, *Winnie the Pooh*, and all the verses of 'The Red Flag'. Dill is not quite so full of beans: she has circles under her eyes – from worrying all night, or so she says.

'A great tribute to my professional powers. I can take care of myself, you know.'

She replies that I may know plenty about shape-shifting, spell-design and the conversion of inconvenient people into stone, but I am as a babe in the woods when it comes to survival in your high-technology elective dictatorship.

'So who was it undid the electronic handcuffs when we were doing our Slave Labour stint? I learn fast.'

Small potatoes, she says, compared to halloo-ing to my old chum through a cordon of MI-something storm troopers.

'Hardly noticed them,' I say, and swagger through an account of our nifty departure from the Tattoo. Then I realize what is really bothering her: I have just spent the night with Albanna.

Better leave me to make my explanations.

*

The PM's gut reaction, when the runaway returns, may be a maternal impulse to embrace first, smack second and ask questions afterwards. But whatever her emotions (if any), she suppresses them with her usual efficiency: the briefing documents have made it clear that ancient Celts are hot-blooded, quick to take the huff, and better handled with the softest of kid gloves. So a very friendly fuss is made, and no questions are asked (while back in town the security services interrogate the waiter from Café Listeria within an inch of his life).

'How delightful to have you back so soon,' beams the PM, ever the accomplished hostess. 'You must be famished. Would you care for a little bite to eat?'

Albanna confesses to a slight peckishness.

An ambitious backbencher has sent down some grouse, bagged during his time-share week at the Saudi-Swiss Consolidated Grouse Moor beyond the Great Glen. Can she be tempted? And perhaps some cold poached wild salmon to toy with while the birds are cooked? And, if she has a corner left, she might care to finish up with the Debriefing Centre's own Top Secret Recipe whisky trifle (never yet successfully copied, decoded or leaked). She agrees to all the above, but asks that it be supplemented with a few delicacies from the nearest Chinese take-away. Motorcycle dispatch riders roar off to do her bidding.

As the silver salvers roll in on trolleys, propelled by licensed-to-kill agents trained in French service, the PM apologizes for leaving Albanna to lunch alone. Government business calls: a fact-finding mission to survey an abandoned factory. She'll tell her guest all about it when they return at tea time. In the meanwhile, Albanna need not feel lonely: a scurry of junior ministers and Scottish Office minions will stay behind to keep her company. And, should her guardians' conversation pall, she might care to screen more of the videotapes prepared by the Media Ministry for her delectation, explaining life in modern Greater Britain plc.

'Well, that was a damp squib,' says the Secretary of State for Style as the official cars whisk down the motorway that has been emptied for their exclusive use. The tawse factory at Lochgelly seems to have vanished without trace.

'We may have to rely on cheap Far Eastern imports,' ventures the Chancellor. 'At least until we can attract sufficient foreign investment to set up a plant of our own.'

'Never!' declares the Prime Minister, with a vehemence that startles her companions. 'If you have done your homework, you will recall that Clause 19 of the Public Flogging Bill specifies that all implements will be of British patent and manufacture. And this is no mere kneejerk protectionist gesture. Once upon a time, before the namby-pamby soaking wet socialist rot set in, Great Britain led the world in corporal punishment technology. And I have vowed that we shall do so once again!'

Two days later the government party, with Albanna in tow, heads south for the capital. I swither, wondering if I ought to follow; I can keep an eye on her perfectly well from here, but it might be safer to be close at hand, to take preventive action in case of any queenly clangers. But I postpone the trip, preoccupied with domestic matters. Even the star magician of the tribe is entitled to a little private life. Especially when Dill and I have come to the mutual conclusion that it's time to start living together.

The decision, I should confess, is not entirely our own. When Dill brings us back to the tower block to collect some clean clothes for the twins, I find an official-looking document dangling from the letter box. It states that since, after two nights' absence, I have obviously found alternative accommodation, my flat is being reallocated to a more deserving tenant, at a commercially adjusted rent.

It takes little time to pack. The household, before my arrival, was not exactly overendowed with worldly goods. Most of what we own is manufactured from spells and shadows, easy to dismantle and reassemble at a new location. The rest fits into five large Mothercare bags.

*

'Our ways are not their ways,' explains the Minister for the Family. 'Their ways are perfectly all right, of course, in their proper place, which is several thousand miles from here.'

'You see,' explains the PM to Albanna, who is being treated to a view of the Cabinet at work, 'we're sending them all back where they came from. We cannot allow ourselves to be swamped any further by alien cultures.'

'They have many sterling qualities,' observes the Secretary of State for Style, 'but you should see their taste in wallpaper.' He shudders.

'We had the foresight to nip the problem in the bud,' declares Albanna. 'We established forts on all the high places, commanding the sea coasts and the estuaries. And on the landward side we put up a nice sturdy wall, to exercise stringent immigration controls and keep out the southern hordes.'

'With all due respect,' interpolates the Media Minister, 'we rather imagined the wall was built by the Romans.'

'Well, they did put up some of the money and personnel, as I recall, but that hardly entitles them to claim all the credit. Take my advice, be wary of foreign investors.'

'But did it work?' asks the Minister for the Family, somewhat shaky on anything before 1066.

Albanna's gaze travels round the long table, giving each of her listeners a long, searching scrutiny. 'Apparently not.'

The launch of Albanna is carefully planned by the Secretary of State for Style and his team of freelance consultants. The resulting bluster and ballyhoo succeeds in pushing an inconvenient collection of gas, radiation and security leaks right off the front pages. The tabloids, by Prime Ministerial diktat, make much of her. Everybody loves a Royal.

She appears at significant sporting events and at Command Performances, where an aide whispers explanations of the jokes told by toothy celebrities in luminous jackets. She opens a new wing in a private hospital, reviews – with a faintly puzzled air – a military regiment, and is seen enjoying a joke with a champion racehorse, owned by the Queen. She is also the subject of feverish speculation. The world wonders: Is she married? Where is her treasure buried? Does she have any more tattoos?

Her minders are not profligate in granting interviews, but they are clever. They allow one brief televised *tête-à-tête*. Her questioner is an old veteran of conversations with Royals and other fabled beasts; he is a master of hushed tones, gravitas, and the deferential smile. The subjects have been decided well in advance. For three exasperating days, Albanna's watchdogs have drilled her in the correct responses. She is exhorted to limit her conversation to her amazement at modern technology, her views on contemporary fashions, and her favourite sports. Her public will be thrilled to know that she shares her modern counterpart's love of the equestrian arts.

The ten-minute chat rolls smoothly, with no surprises, until she confides that, next to horse-racing, she loves wrestling best. Turning to face the camera, she issues a public challenge to both Queen and Prime Minister to grapple with her in a field of mud: winner of three falls takes the realm. With many hours of skilful editing, this nugget is extracted from the tape: no one would have been so foolish as to unleash her live.

The glossy magazines and colour supplements queue for her attentions. Albanna appears on four covers in a single month, upstaging a TV soap star's divorce and a pregnant Princess. Each publication finds its particular angle:

Beauty Secrets of the Ancient Britons

Siege Cuisine: The Ultimate Dinner Party

The Free-Market Answer to Juvenile Crime: How We Solved Our Hooligan Problem and Boosted Exports

A Tomb of My Own

Albanna also fires the imagination of the Culture lobby. A cartel of Corporate Patrons of the Arts sets a competition, with a hefty prize, for a new opera on the theme Britannia Revived. A television production company signs her up as technical adviser on a new eleven-part Celtic costume drama: 'The Mist and the Mistletoe'. Book publishers clamour to get in on the act, dreaming of lavishly illustrated full-colour coeditions with TV tie-ins and minimal text. But most of them come a cropper. *Treasures of a Queen* founders when Albanna refuses to reveal even one of the many sites where she's hidden her booty. *Royal Gardening Tips* looks rocky when Albanna insists that the only proper fertilizer is a human sacrifice. *The Ancient Celtic Kitchen* seems promising, in outline form, until a home economist attempts to test out recipes that begin 'Open the vein of a tethered bullock . . .' Another project, *Before Balmoral: Home Life among Scotland's Iron Age Royals*, excites considerable interest until Albanna provides a few details of her own domestic arrangements. The editorial conference comes to a swift, embarrassed termination, and the whole idea is quietly dropped.

I know my Albanna; she can work the crowd with the best of them. So I am hardly surprised at the explosion of public interest in this colourful new celebrity. In the popular press, simple time-lines and maps have helped to explain her origins. According to the latest surveys, an impressive thirty-three per cent of the English population now accepts that the world did not begin in 1066, although twenty-six per cent still believes that Scotland wakes from its enchanted sleep only to supply the telly programmes for New Year's Eve.

The PM is pleased with her guest's progress. She decides that a little joint exposure will be good for both of them. So she decides to bring Albanna along, as cheerleader and support band, when she addresses the opening rally for the massive Tribute to the British Family. Pious pop stars, a tame bishop, captains of industry, marketing gurus, and the spokeswoman from the ruling Party's House and Home section feature on the programme.

Before setting out for the spanking new Conference Centre on the site of the old London University, the PM makes time for a quick briefing session, to ensure that Albanna's views are sound:

'And how do you feel about The Family?'

'May the Goddess bless it.'

'You did, of course, have families back then?'

'How could you doubt it? Woe betide the child who does not know its lineage, unto the twentieth generation.'

'Good. So you appreciated their importance to a well-ordered society.'

'The family is the very spine and belly of the tribe.'

'Excellent. Well, I think we see eye to eye on this. Just say all that to the audience.'

Nevertheless, she calls in the Minister for the Family and advises him that Albanna's slot on the programme should be kept short and sweet.

'Everything is under control, ma'am. You'll make the keynote address, after which we wheel on Albanna in tandem with the Motherhood expert, and you all do a quick three-hander: chaired by your good self. I'm certain you'll have no difficulty in retaining the upper hand.'

The PM is satisfied. If she can keep several hundred unruly ex-schoolboys quivering in their pinstripes at her every word, she should be able to manage this refugee from a sword-and-sorcery comic book.

Unsurprisingly, the PM's speech inspires tumultuous applause. She is in the company of her most adoring followers. When the hubbub subsides she introduces Albanna, 'who will speak to us of family life in a time far less affluent than our own, when everyone pulled together, knew who was boss, were unafraid to take responsibility for their own actions and didn't shy away from a little hard work.'

'Just the other day,' confides the PM to the crowd, 'Albanna and I were talking about the great traditions of the British family. And do you know that even then, in an age that we might imagine – with all due respect – to be more primitive than our own, the family was perceived as the cornerstone of society. And what she said has confirmed our belief that people don't really change much from one age to the next – not if they are good people, with good, sound values . . . like our own!'

Invited to address the gathering, Albanna proves herself word-perfect – as befitting one brought up in the oral tradition – in repeating the remarks that so delighted the PM. When the warm applause and well-bred cheers have died away, the PM invites the Motherhood specialist to expound on his new bestseller: *The Mother as Moral Guardian*. As he warms to his theme – a statistical analysis of the social havoc wrought by women who let their marriages break down – Albanna looks increasingly perplexed.

Finally, she can contain her puzzlement no longer, and interrupts. 'Marriage?' she asks. 'You keep going on about marriage. What exactly is it?'

To the tune of several thousand mildly scandalized titters, the PM and the expert strive to explain the meaning of the word.

'That's disgusting!' Albanna bellows. 'You mean women and men actually living together . . . in the same settlement, the same houses, the same BEDS??? Cohabiting with each other throughout the lunar cycle? That's abnormal! Perverted! Mating with the opposite sex for purposes of procreation is a necessary chore for the child-hungry, but surely nobody does it for pleasure! Or hangs about when the job is done! What kind of family life do you call that??'

The PM, goggle-eyed, leans forward to interrupt the flow. Albanna reaches out and claps a tattooed hand over the Prime Ministerial mouth.

'We all know', she announces, 'that babies have to be made, but there is only one decent way to do it. When we know our fertile time has come, we send a message to the males on the other side of the river. We arrange a meeting-place, have a gargantuan feast and try not to annoy each other to the point of violence, then go off into the trees to do the needful. Then we all head home again to our separate settlements, happy that we have fulfilled our obligations to the Goddess of Fertility. I must say, I am shocked to discover how far your people have deviated from the norm. You should be ashamed of yourselves!'

The PM signals frantically to someone offstage, and the curtain is pulled. Delegates are invited to adjourn for an early lunch break, to be followed by an address from a prominent American evangelist on the theme 'Purging Parental Permissiveness: And The Children's Teeth Shall Be Set On Edge'.

*

'It can't be true!' storms the PM during the hastily organized Cabinet postmortem. 'Get a historian to check the facts.'

'Most of them work in Australia and America now, ma'am,' explains the Minister for the Family. 'Ever since we closed the uneconomic university departments.'

'Find one. Even if you have to ship him over from Yale or wherever. But just make sure he is One of Us. Tell him there's a knighthood in it. But come hell or high water, I want those outrageous claims refuted.'

'We may be on rather shaky ground there. The period in question suffers from a dearth of documentary evidence. The nearest thing to a reliable historical source, unfortunately, is Albanna herself.'

'Then get someone to rewrite the history,' snaps the PM. 'It won't be the first time . . .'

'Perhaps the moment has come', ventures the Chancellor of the Exchequer, 'to drop the lady from the menu. She's turning out to be more of a liability than an asset . . .'

'Not yet.' The PM guillotines the suggestion with a midair karate chop. 'She has enormous potential, if properly handled, as a potent symbol of British Supremacy. Which could be very useful if those European human rights johnnies don't stop nipping at our heels.'

'I suggest', ventures the Secretary of State for Style, 'that we concentrate on visual exploitation. Trot her out in full battledress, helmet and spear and all, on appropriate occasions – but keep the chat to a bare minimum.'

'And for goodness' sake', pleads the Scottish Colonial Governor, 'keep her down South. I've already heard rumours that certain elements in the lunatic nationalist fringe are taking her up as some kind of symbol . . .'

His boss withers him with a glance. 'Don't be so damp. All the more reason to parade her as a BRITISH figurehead. And I don't think you need to worry unduly about your little tartan patriots. Those people are addicted to lost causes. In fact, I'd be very pleased to rub their faces in it, so I suggest we consider sending her back up there for a Scottish tour at the earliest opportunity. Suitably chaperoned, of course, and well wrapped up in the Union Jack!'

*

Dill is worried about money. She finds this a new experience. Her medical qualification, as well as giving her status, prestige, and the imagined power of a minor demigod, was supposed to provide a meal ticket for life.

I find it hard to understand why she won't let me exercise a little legerdemain on her behalf with a counterfeit cash card: if I can move a mountain (well, all right, it was only a small hill) to terrify an enemy invader, I should be able to fabricate a slice of plastic and a magic number that is never out of credit.

I tell her she suffers from a misplaced moral sense. Banks, as she has repeatedly informed me, are rarely on the side of the angels. If I choose one that is particularly pernicious in its entanglements – investments in armaments, South African slave mines and assorted planet-poisoning enterprises – she can count every punched-in request for cash as another blow against the armies of the Right.

She counters with a lecture on ethics and a tour round the Calvinist guilt complex. I reply that all these notions have come after my time: from where I sit they are mere passing fads, like monotheism or nouvelle cuisine.

But then she puts it another way, which I understand better. She needs, so she claims, to practise her trade.

This I understand. I grow twitchy if I let more than a week elapse without working some little spell or token metamorphosis. Fortunately, with the twins to feed, clothe, and civilize, my skills have little risk of rusting. But Dill sits in a cleft stick of her own choosing: she refuses to become financially dependent on me (this scruple is entirely outside my experience; where I come from, life is a daisy chain of power games and bids for patronage) but she has very little hope of another job in the health-care industry. If a convicted, window-smashing lesbian lefty isn't on one of those officially nonexistent employers' blacklists, then I'm the secretary of the Edinburgh South Conservative Ladies' Guild.

She comes up with her own solution. So we zip the twins into their anoraks and head for the Souk. Those familiar with Edinburgh from an earlier, more expansive age will remember the site as the long flight of stone steps leading down from Princes Street to Waverley Station. But no trains stop here any more. The rolling stock – or those remnants not yet ready for the scrapheap in the year of the great railway sell-off – now carries wealthy tourists through the Caledonian Reservation on the Victorian Tartan Heritage run or the 1920s Murder Mystery Fundays.

The steps are ankle-deep in litter. The inhabitants of the sleeping bags and cardboard shelters clustered near the bottom of the stairs are exercising their freedom of choice: No Poll Tax, No Rubbish Collection, says the local franchise-holder of Urban Maintenance Services plc.

'It's your privilege to make your own alternative cleansing arrangements,' chirrups the clerk behind the shatterproof glass barrier at Accounts Receivable, mentally calculating the Incentive Bonus she will receive for Man Hours Saved.

Further up the stone steps, small adventurous enterprises struggle to take root. The Colonial Governor's heart, in the unlikely event of a visit, should be gladdened. A redundant dental technician (bridges and crowns are for the privileged few, who now pick them up in Singapore along with their hand-tailored suits) applies her sculptural skills to the manufacture of small wax replicas of prominent government figures. She offers a discount to customers who supply their own pins. Mass production is possible: the favourites never seem to change.

Nearby, a psychiatric nurse (thrown out of work when his bemused charges were cast out into the arms of the warm and caring community) supplies a listening ear to all comers, for a modest fee. A competitor, across the way, sells therapeutic mantras: 'The Universe won't change, friend. Change yourself.'

On the next landing, a pair of specialists offer reading and writing services to the astigmatic and the short-sighted, who could as easily afford a Porsche as a pair of spectacles. Elsewhere roaring trades are conducted in the sale of outdated foods and damaged tins, candles made from nubs of soap, and second-hand umbrellas; cheap earrings glitter from one stall, wholemeal pasties glower from another. Most popular of all is a little stand run by an old acquaintance of ours. Ms L-O-V-E & H-A-T-E, who did time with us on the dear old Slave Labour scheme, now stands proudly before a board of devastating political caricatures: a gloomy Chancellor, a cringing Colonial Governor, a simpering Minister for Patriotism. The artist can hardly keep up with demand – as fast as she pins a new one up on the board, someone rushes over to buy it. We buy a realistic sketch of the PM as a carrion crow, to decorate our bathroom wall.

In the midst of all these activities, a grizzled, headbanded man stands in a cloud of patchouli oil, holding a mouth organ and a battered guitar. He earns a healthy income by not singing old Bob Dylan songs: traders, residents, and passers-by alike all pay handsomely for his silence.

Into this little hive of commerce we descend with the twinlets. Dill orders them to keep their light fingers firmly in their pockets, on pain of being left behind. I foresee another argument about discipline brewing up by tea time.

'Hi-ya!'

We see two more familiar faces: our fellow jailbirds with the flowery tattoos – my ex-neighbour Kerry, and her friend Marie.

'I heard you've moved out of Colditz. And how's the pair of wee horrors? Do you girls want to come and play with my Diana again soon? She's got another new doll. She loves it. It says swearie words when you push a button. It's a scream. So where are you staying now, Gwhyldis?'

Dill answers for me. 'With me.'

Kerry and Marie, beaming, exchange sharp elbows in the ribs.

'And when did you move in?' asks Marie.

'Late August.'

'Oh, very nice!' She turns to Kerry. 'That'll be a fiver you owe me, doll. I said it wouldn't take a month.'

'Congratulations,' says Kerry. 'You know your old house? They've let it to an old boy who's crammed in seven lodgers.'

'In a one-bedroom flat?'

'Someone sleeps in the bath. He makes them clear out at 6 a.m. every morning, so the Government Snoopers don't cotton on. And what brings you pair to Edinburgh's Shopper's Paradise?'

'I'm thinking of setting up a tent,' says Dill. 'Cut-price medical care.'

'That's great,' says Marie. 'This dump could use a doctor. And we'll be colleagues. Kerry and I are running a stall selling condoms and other safe sex aids. We've got them in fashion colours.'

'Given up the game?' asks Dill.

'Well, that's a long story, hen. Got time for a wee coffee?'

We repair to the nearby Café Carmen Miranda, a tropical paradise of painted pineapples, high camp parrots, and primary colours concealed beyond an austere Georgian façade. The twins disappear behind towering slabs of Black Forest gateau.

'And so,' says Marie, licking the froth from her cappuccino, 'after I came out of hospital, we decided to press charges. We knew who the bastards were.'

'And you know what the judge said when it came to trial? That we were asking for it. What did we expect? So he found them not guilty. Then sweetie-pie here stands up in the courtroom and starts shouting him down. Says that he wouldn't be so soft on some bastard who smashed a shop window and nicked the goods.'

'What happened?'

'Mrs Pankhurst here gets fined for contempt of court, that's what. At least she didn't get sent back for another dose of Slave Labour like the last time.'

'Oh, and I forget to tell you – guess who the Judge was? Our old pal Corbiestane.'

'Thought the whole thing was a great giggle. Could hardly keep his face straight for the whole five minutes. Wound up giving us one of those oily smiles and saying in his bools-in-the-mooth voice that ladies would do better keeping off the streets at night. Case dismissed.'

That evening, while strolling home from his Lodge meeting, Lord Corbiestane has an unpleasant surprise. As he rounds the corner of Queen Street Gardens, he utters an undignified cry: he turns to face the impudent person who has just pinched his titled bottom, and finds only empty air. Nevertheless, as he quickens his pace, he hears footsteps close behind him. Without benefit of any visible owner, they follow him all the way to his front door. When he is safely locked and bolted in, the faithful hound who waits on his elegant staircase sets up an appalled Baskervillean howl. His wife's two Siamese, perched on the banisters, arch their backs and hiss at something over his left shoulder. Booting all three creatures with true judicial impartiality, he heads for the telephone, then thinks again. Any fate is better than that of laughing stock. As he climbs to his bedroom, the footsteps come with him. He will just have to get used to them: from now on he'll never walk alone.

Something has scared off all the birds at the time-share grouse moor. In the lodge, a succession of cries not only curdles the blood but freezes the bathwater of this week's proud proprietors. Wooden wheels rumble past the dining-room windows, stopping dead a conversation already flagging, since no one has a bag to brag about. Curses, thuds and whinnies resound in the rose garden.

In her attic bedroom, a young waitress prepares to liven up the proceedings by painting her face with lightning-flashes, snakes and spirals, a trick she learned in a previous job. She doesn't care if they sack her; she's already bought her bus ticket and is away home to Glasgow in the morning. But when she makes her entrance into the drawing-room, wheeling in the trolley of coffee and cigars, no one notices: the guests are staring in hypnotized horror as the tartan carpet is rucked and rumpled by an invisible pair of grunting wrestlers.

She is annoyed at this upstaging. 'See those Picts, they never know when to stop. One little victory over the Romans, and they think they're Tarzan.'

She stomps to the French windows, flings them wide, and bellows into the darkness: 'Hey, you lot! The party's over. Go home and give the rest of us a bit of peace. You've already won!'

Silence falls. The carpet smoothes and lies flat.

She turns to the gape-mouthed company. They have noticed her now.

'I had a Hieland grannie,' she confides. 'I can see things.'

CHAPTER FIVE

DILL'S HEALTH TENT is the hit of the Souk. The queues wind up and down the steps, and run along Princes Street as far as the Scott monument. She is forced, much to her mortification, to institute a conventional appointments system. I, as a mark of my devotion, agree to play the classic role of dragon-lady receptionist. It's a dirty job, but someone has to do it. Besides, I can take care of the minor ailments myself, with a few murmured incantations, saving everybody's time.

At Dill's insistence, every spell is accompanied by a bottle of placcbos (pure vitamin C, minus label) so people don't get the wrong impression, and think we're doing miracle cures. I keep telling her there is nothing miraculous about them, but for a professional healer she shows remarkably little curiosity about my methods. I don't know why my beloved is so prickly about these matters: sometimes I think she is more old-fashioned than I am. However, I try to avoid trivial quarrels, since I need to marshal my spiritual energies. Albanna is coming back to town.

Kerry and Marie keep me posted on news from my old neighbourhood. Behind his permanently boarded windows, the grocer has stuck new price labels on the milk cartons.

'Not my fault,' he explains to a queue of aggrieved shoppers. 'They've slapped on a new radioactivity-testing tax. Nothing I can do about it. If you don't like it, buy a cow of your own.'

Thanks to developments such as these, our surgery sees a colourful range of cases: malnutrition is popular once again, and industrial injuries display a curious lack of old-fashioned blood and gore. Very little surprises us: me because I can see it coming, Dill because she is rapidly losing her capacity for astonishment, although I'm glad to say her talent for outrage is holding firm. However, one new patient does give her pause for thought. She mentions it on the Number 23 bus going home, on our way to collect the twins from nursery school (wangling them a place took more magic than turning back the Romans, I promise you).

'Did you see that woman who came in this afternoon? Between the two bronchitises and the waiter with food poisoning?'

'Of course. I see everybody, don't I? The pale one, with the bad dust allergy.'

'That's her. She wasn't just pale; she was transparent.'

'What did you expect? She's a ghost.'

Dill just looks at me. Sometimes I despair.

'Do you seriously think I'm the only aberration in town? How long have you lived in this city?'

'Since I was a student . . .'

'And you're seriously telling me she's the first one you've met?'

She bridles. 'How should I know? People don't usually come up to you at parties and say Hi, I'm the Spectre of the Canongate, do they?'

'I wouldn't know. We haven't been to any. When we do get an invitation, you turn it down.'

She ignores this. I must remember to pursue it further.

After all this time in Edinburgh, I would think she would have learned one thing: there are people living in these old stone tenements who have always been here. All she has to do is look around her.

Do you see those three grim-faced matrons in felt hats, getting off the bus at Victoria Street? They're heading down to the Grassmarket to see a witch-burning: they never miss one. That man with the stick, limping past Greyfriars, hurt his leg at Flodden; it gives him bother in wet weather. Along the Cowgate, the barmaids grumble with the regulars about the rising price of beer. You can hear the brewer's drayhorse on the cobblestones. Over the road, at the concert hall that used to be a kirk, a black-gowned minister floats up through the floorboards to disapprove of the rehearsals. In a Princes Street shop, a headless queen wanders wistfully through the millinery department. And down at the Tron a mob is gathering, angry at some new outrage by the State. It could be any time.

To the discomfiture of the Colonial Governor and the satisfaction of the PM (who sometimes likes to see her minions turn slowly, slowly in the wind) a Scottish tour is quickly organized for Albanna. Plenty of photo opportunities, but with mouth firmly glued shut, comes the directive from on high. The Colonial Governor, the Secretary of State for Style, and the Minister for Patriotism are put in charge. They sink into deep armchairs at the Minister's club to discuss this poisoned chalice.

'You do the visit to the salmon farm, there's a good fellow. I hate the smell of fish.'

'With pleasure — as long as you take over the unveiling of the fibreglass cromlech in the shopping centre at that depressing new town.'

'Glasgow needs a bit of fiddling. The Chamber of Commerce actually wants her to talk to them, God help us.'

'Say yes. No problem. She'll never get a word in edgeways.'

'Then there's the appearance on ASLEC . . .'

'ASLEC?'

'The local telly station: Australo-Scottish Light Entertainment Channel. They plumped for a celebrity chat programme, but we thought that spelled trouble, so we've held out for a game show instead.'

'Is that wise, old man? Trying to explain the rules of one of those damn things to the Ancient Celt?'

'She's not a contestant, you fool, she's handing out the prizes. The top whack is a new sports car — they thought they'd deck it out like an old war chariot, for a bit of a giggle.'

'As long as she doesn't use the opportunity to sneak in a speech . . .'

'Not with that presenter, darling — and anyway, it's on tape.'

'Now, how shall we divide up the other outings? In Aberdeen, she's opening Ye Olde Texan Oil Town Nostalgia Park on the site of a redundant shipyard. Then it's up to some godforsaken derelict village in Sutherland to see an interesting little enterprise called The

Crofter's Cottage Genealogy Centre that seems to be pulling in the Yanks and Canadians like billyo. Finally down to Edinburgh, to launch the new North British Heritage Centre on the Royal Mile.'

'I think it might be a good idea if we both turned up at that one. It's bound to be high-profile – best not to let any slips show in sight of the Boss. Then, before the caravan moves south again, I've got another possible appearance lined up for the old girl. Can't give you all the details yet, but it's a corker.'

'Will it make the front pages?'

'I sincerely hope not. But it should make history – of a kind.'

The reason for the Colonial Governor's reticence is the vow he took in his youth to keep all Lodge secrets locked in his bosom – lest said bosom be torn open by silver knife and its enclosed heart duly fed to the ocean fishes. The Secretary of State for Style has many sterling qualities, but membership in the Druidicals is not among them. He has apparently risen to his present eminence by other means. Therefore the Colonial Governor cannot divulge the exciting news of the debate now raging in the Edinburgh Innermost Temple Number 3: Should the Brotherhood break with sacred tradition and invite to dinner the closest living link with the ancient Bards – in spite of her inconvenient extra chromosome?

Female persons have never been allowed into the sanctum. They may cook the feasts, and wash the ceremonial dishes afterwards, but their presence in the actual Chamber would be tantamount to pollution. Even the PM herself, in the full panoply of her might and splendour, is barred from entry. However, should her spouse belong (and he may well hold membership in some southern branch), she would be welcome to bake a cake for the Archdruid's Retirement Fund Tombola.

Nevertheless, some of the younger, more progressive members feel that Albanna's presence would give an imprimatur of Celtic authenticity to their proceedings, to the immeasurable enhance-ment of druidical prestige. Surely, they argue, her probable age – not to mention her royal blood and tattooed skin – unsexes her. But their elders shake their heads, and cite the relevant strictures in the old manuals of the fraternity. They hesitate to express the real reason for their resistance: the well-founded fear that, after one glance at their supposedly antique rites and regalia, the old girl would blow the gaff.

Shortly after his colloquy with the Secretary of State for Style, the Colonial Governor flies north to put his case for the invitation. In the anteroom he removes his suit jacket, puts on an exotically embroidered ritual pinafore, and rolls up his right shirtsleeve to expose one bony elbow. Together with the Brethren, he queues up in order of rank to kneel before the portrait of the order's legendary Founder: a handsome, blond King Arthur, in dark Victorian oils, gazing into the glorious future that lies beyond his gilded frame.

The burled walnut doors (bequest of a long-gone West Lothian industrialist, whose factories have followed him into oblivion) close solemnly behind the Druids. Far be it from me, with my unfair advantage, to tattle on their deliberations. The eloquent arguments, on both sides of the question, have been interred in their secret archives. But let it be said that a compromise is reached. Albanna will not be allowed into the Chamber, but will be invited to take part in a ritual that is, perforce, more public. By a lucky coincidence, she is scheduled to arrive in Edinburgh on the day before the Winter Solstice, when the Brotherhood will once more perform its vigil on Arthur's Seat.

The decision to welcome Albanna into this sacred circle is one vote short of unanimous. Mr Melville, unaccountably, demurs. But since, in a recent election, he has been deposed as Archdruid, his dissent counts for very little. The Colonial Governor retires to telephone his colleagues, and informs the Secretary and the Minister that he now stands corrected: this historic event should make the papers after all.

If the Solstice is coming, so is Christmas. The twins, corrupted at nursery school, present us with a list of non-negotiable demands. Dill has to be forcibly restrained from throttling them.

'I am not buying them a Kiddies' Chemical Warfare Set. Nor a simpering, disembodied head to be permed and lipsticked. Nor (even if we had the money, which we don't) a pint-sized battery-driven Porsche. I don't care if every other brat in the class is getting one!'

I try to explain that children, now as always, hate to be different from their peers: this peculiarity, indeed, extends to their elders. When shrewdly handled, the quirk has given several hundred generations of political and religious con-artists their chance to seize power. Dill says that is no reason to condone it, and refuses to allow any of the aforementioned goodies to darken our door. As an alternative, she suggests a selection of improving picture books, instructive wall-friezes and ideologically correct fairy tales. I remind her that the last of these have not been available for some time, thanks to market forces and the Official Viewpoints Act.

To forestall arguments, tears and tantrums on all sides, I announce that the holiday is coming early in our house, and present the girls with a particularly wonderful kitten. But I do wish Dill would not keep interrogating me about where it came from. She suspects that it has not originated from any of the usual sources, especially when she sees it capering through the bathroom wall.

'Couldn't you at least conjure up one that pees in the litter tray instead of on the floor?'

'A cat's a cat,' I tell her. 'Count yourself lucky the girls didn't ask for a wolf.'

As she spreads out a newspaper to blot up the kitten's latest mistake, a familiar face smiles up at us.

'It's Albanna!' she cries, lifting up the soggy sheet. 'She's back in Scotland.'

'I knew that.'

'Did you see this?'

'I do have other channels of information.'

'All right then, smartarse, so I suppose you already know she is coming to Edinburgh this afternoon to attend the official opening of the new North British – Goddess help us – Heritage Centre.'

'It was inevitable.'

'The festivities are open to the public. Wouldn't you like to go?'

'Not particularly. But why don't you take the twins? I'm sure they'd adore it.'

I have no desire to stand in a milling throng of onlookers while the great and the famous pass by. If I can't be one of the stars, I'd rather not be part of the show. Besides, I am planning my own reunion with the lady. In private. And there are one or two arrangements to be made.

'If I'm not here when you get back,' I say, 'don't worry. I'll turn up sooner or later. And tell you everything.'

'I'm not sure I want to hear it,' says Dill, wrestling the girls into their anoraks. 'You know I don't trust that woman.'

'Very wise,' I reply.

Just as I expected, Dill and the girls are confined with several hundred other punters behind police barriers while television cameras and security men jockey for strategic positions around the distinguished guests. Albanna, flanked by the two Cabinet Ministers, has topped up her tattoos with some flamboyant touches of face paint. She also wears a surprisingly conventional Royal hat, and seems to have been taking lessons from Someone in the queenly art of handbag-carrying. Brandishing her celebrated spear (Mr Melville, seeing the news pictures later, winces), she cuts the ribbon and declares the Heritage Centre open for business.

Before she can launch into a speech or an outpouring of declamatory verse, she is hustled through the open turnstiles for a private tour of the premises. A few minutes later, the watching public is invited to queue up, pay its admission fees, and follow – at a respectful distance – in the Royal footsteps.

Dill is not nearly as enthusiastic as the twins when it comes time to climb into the giant wheeled sporrans for the Journey Through Auld Lang Syne. The hushed, reverential tones of an out-of-fashion actor, breathlessly grateful for the work, ushers the time-travellers on their voyage of discovery. As the sporranmobiles trundle from one exhibit to the next, little twinnish fingers reach out to test the texture of a washable megalith, and tiny throats emit identical screams of glee while rolling past a scene of sacrifice, where a trussed-up victim waits to be pushed into a peat bog by a priestly hand. Roman soldiers, armed with an eagle standard, bear down on the painted stage-flat of the Antonine Wall, to the tune of tape-recorded marching feet.

In a native settlement (someone's done some crafty research) a full-sized model of Albanna stands with folded arms, receiving tribute from her crouching subjects: I am sure the honoured guest will be pleased by this tableau, since the artist has awarded her an extra, unmerited five inches of height. Presumably, she sat as the sculptor's model: those tattoos, and the imperious expression, are taken from the life. The twins are unimpressed, never having met the lady (who didn't even have the grace to send up something for their Solstice stockings), but they perk up further down the line, where Saint Columba, looking pious, paddles his coracle across a pool of real water. The girls contemplate a refreshing dip, but Dill deters them with a threat of no ice cream later.

Kenneth Macalpine's coronation, as king over all the Picts and Scots, does not excite the girls; John Knox makes them nervous; Mary Queen of Scots, approaching the block, is swiftly upstaged by her little dog. Her son, James VI, leading his caravan of eager nobles south to claim the English Crown, scans the painted bridge across the River Tweed and licks his lips.

At this point the trundling sporrans pick up speed, as if reluctant to dwell upon the events that follow. The girls look queasy. The smug smile on the face of the Duke of Argyll, caught in the moment of signing the Act of Union, would disappear in a flash if he were but flesh, as both twins lean over to be copiously carsick upon his breeches. Dill ignores the scandalized murmurs from the sporrans behind her own, and tidies up small mouths with plenty of tissues and an almost-maternal pride.

She is too busy soothing the twins with peppermints to notice much of what is left of the exhibition, until a jaunty fiddle tune announces the end of the tour, and the sporrans disgorge their victims into the Heritage Centre Souvenir Shop. By the time Dill has prised the girls away from the Adam-style neoclassical dolls' house, and removed a selection of tasteful coffee mugs, lavender sachets, and repro Celtic brooches from their persons, she notices that all is not as it should be behind the cash desks.

The shop assistants, in pert plaid uniforms, ignore the customers altogether, and murmur excitedly among themselves. Presenting herself at the till with two little bags of Auntie Jeannie's Authentic Highland Butterscotch Toffee (her bribe to keep the twins from filching further), Dill struggles to attract their attention. The one whose eye she catches looks faintly resentful at being torn from the chat, but remembers just in time that the Customer Comes First. She apologizes for her distraction, and explains that the extraordinary events of the last twenty minutes have given the staff quite a nasty turn.

'She was standing right there, I saw her myself. About to make her mark as the first guest in the Visitors' Book – just an X really; they say she can't write even if she is a Queen. Then all of a sudden, she's gone. You'll see when you go outside – they're blocking off the whole of the High Street, and all the closes up and down. There's nothing official yet, but the security guard thinks she's been kidnapped by terrorists. It's a shame – they've cancelled the Sherry Reception in the directors' office. I wonder what they'll do with all that cake?'

The Grand Opening of the North British Heritage Centre is not the only escorted tour through time taking place today in the High Street. Less well publicized, and perhaps less alluring to those seeking educational fun for all the family, is the warren of buried lanes and houses hidden below the City Chambers, itself a museum to the now-defunct institution of local government . . .

Down in Mary King's Close, a small party of urban archaeologists, clairvoyants, and aficionados of the bizarre negotiate the steep, cobbled passageways, crouch under low lintels, and tread carefully to avoid stirring up the dust for fear of whatever antique germs might still be lurking there. Led by a voluble local historian, they climb sixteenth-century stairways leading nowhere, peer into paneless windows, pass bakers' ovens long grown cold. By the light of torches, they trace the outlines of painted flowers on a wall and the spyholes in the doors of suspicious citizens.

Hollowed-out houses, back to back, lead them from one sealed-up street to another: here a pious magistrate hid his skeleton keys, and the spoils of his midnight thieving; there a butcher slaughtered his beasts, and hung their carcases on the hooks suspended from the vaulted ceiling. Someone in the group, sensitive to such things, claims to hear the bellowing of bullocks. The guide describes the hauntings he has seen or heard of: the unidentified face exposed by a camera's flash, the panting of an invisible dog, the sudden trickle of cold sweat on a psychic tourist's palms, the rustling sound behind a fireplace where no mouse has found a crumb for upwards of three hundred years. He counts and re-counts the members of the group, less fearful of losing someone in the maze than of finding one person too many.

Questioned closely, he smiles into his beard, claims he keeps an open mind about such matters, and draws their attention to a black crust of crystallized whisky fumes, where the Excise men once impounded smuggled goods. Then he leads his party up the final turnpike stair. The tour is over. Just as the door to this lost world bangs shut behind them, the group jump at the sound of an outraged bellow from the depths.

'An echo from the abattoir, perhaps,' the guide observes, with a wink, but hustles his visitors quickly out of earshot.

And well he might. Down in the close, a barrage of oaths and curses bounces off the timeworn cobblestones. Albanna, for some reason, is deeply annoyed with me.

Arms folded, I lean against a pillar in a long-abandoned alehouse, admiring the familiar spectacle of an outraged Queen in full spate. Stalking from end to end of the barrel-vaulted chamber, she dissects my pedigree and enumerates the vices, crimes, four-legged para-mours and dubious washing habits of my various great-great-grandmothers. Her voice is loud, her phrases are graphic enough to bring a blush to the ears of any listening ghosts, should they be fluent in the ancient Celtic tongue.

The storm subsides. Our invisible eavesdroppers drift away.

'Finished yet?' I ask her.

'How dare you!'

'It's time we talked.'

'You could have waited. We were about to have sherry and cake.'

'And what then? Bundled into a closed car by your watchdogs, and whisked off to your next guest appearance? Reviewing a regiment? Opening a new Japanese factory to be staffed by three security guards and forty robots? Or a cosy weekend with your

Royal counterparts up at Balmoral, blasting birds with thunder-sticks?'

'And what's wrong with any of that? It's what present-day chieftains do.'

'It isn't what you came for. Remember?'

Albanna scowls, and begins trimming her fingernails with her teeth.

'You were supposed to be coming to the aid of your people in their time of need.'

'Quite right, wizard-woman. If you're so clever, just tell me exactly where in this motley population my people are. Exactly which ones am I supposed to be saving? And from what?'

Some things never change. Politicians always need someone like me to do their thinking for them.

'Anyway,' she continues, with that baleful glare that for lesser mortals would mean a one-way trip to the nearest peat bog, 'who dares to say I'm not doing a great deal of good?'

'Oh yes, no doubt about that, is there? The PM herself thinks you're a wonderful asset. Said so herself in Question Time. Helping to put the Great back into Great Britain. I understand they're naming the new generation of armoured police vehicles after you. Not to mention a new whisky blend for the South African export market. You should be proud ... But I hate to tell you this: the world isn't all panelled boardrooms, television hospitality suites, and first-class executive lounges. You should meet some of the people I know ...'

'The world has always had slaves and peasants.'

'And you were one of them, remember? If you hadn't beaten that yellow-haired harridan from across the Forth in the sacred wrestling match, you'd never have been elected Queen.'

'And you'd still be earning your crust raising winds for the fisherfolk if I hadn't sent you off to study with the great sorceresses of the Hog-backed Isle.'

'And if you hadn't, neither of us would be here now, except perhaps as transmigrated parasites on a seagull's wing.'

Albanna sighs. She can't argue with that. She examines her newest bangle – a digital watch.

'This is childish,' she snaps. 'Let's get down to business. Just what do you want?'

'I'm tired of seeing you shaking hands with some vulgar comedian at a Royal Variety Performance, as filmed for the nine o'clock news. Or modelling Celtic Revival costume jewellery for the Sunday supplements. This is not why I went to all that trouble . . .'

'You have absolutely no understanding of tactics. Patience is the name of the game.'

'You've been here since the Summer Solstice. Exactly how much time do you need?'

She stands with arms akimbo – an impressive figure. She is rapidly becoming almost as wide as she is high.

'Just who is the warrior here – you or me? You may cast the runes, and the spells for winning battles, but I'm the one who goes out and does the dirty work.'

This is an old debate. We could be at it for hours. And I'm afraid we will be. But I have not gone to all the trouble of dragging Albanna through hidden trap doors and tunnels for the sake of reviving this endless argument. I try placation. The same spell I use to buy the twins' obedience with instant ice cream can be employed, with minor adjustments, to produce a glass of fine old Amontillado and a slice of Madeira cake.

'There you are. Just as good as anything you'd get at that Heritage Centre reception.'

'The problem', explains Albanna, through a mouthful of buttery crumbs, 'is that I can't decide which one to overthrow.'

'Which what?'

'Which Queen. You'll have noticed – they seem to have two. The one who wears the crowns and costumes, and the one who bosses everyone about – the quaintly titled PM.'

'Ah, yes.'

'The first one appears to be some kind of high priestess. Wanders about waving at people, and putting everyone she meets into an ecstatic trance. And she talks to horses: fancy that old cult lasting all this time! Her claim to the throne is quite bizarre: apparently the succession all depends on who your father was.'

'How on earth does anyone know?'

'I don't think they do it the way we did, Gwhyldis.'

'Oh, come now. Some things never change.'

'No. You don't understand. They don't just come together at the appropriate seasons for breeding. The males and females mingle . . . all the time. I was quite shocked.'

'Not all of them. Some people still maintain decent standards. Your old friend Dr Dillon and I, for instance . . .'

But I don't bother going into my personal affairs. When it comes to other people's lives, your average Queen has an attention span of less than a minute. And Albanna is no exception.

'Anyway,' she continues, 'the second Queen is the one whose throne interests me. She may not call herself by any Royal titles, but you should see the way her minions cringe and grovel. She gets a lot more respect than you lot ever showed me. But she does hold her crown in the same way we did: through ritual combat at regular intervals.'

'And have you thought of challenging her to a duel?'

'Apparently, it isn't quite that simple. The challenger has to come from a certain other tribe.'

'Perhaps you should become a member.'

The possibility does not intrigue her. Apparently she's met them, and was not impressed. 'There are, however, other paths to power. I think she wants me to become an ally. She has offered me a chieftainship that lies within her gift.'

I try to sound impressed. 'How interesting. You must have her worried.'

'It's somewhere in the southlands. For a tribe that seems to be composed mainly of old retired warriors with white moustaches, and smart young persons in very shiny cars. Their last leader has just died – of overfeeding, I think – and she wants me to replace him. Her counsellors think I would be perfect. It's what they call a Safe Seat.'

'No throne is ever safe,' I feel impelled to warn her. 'I hope you told them that.'

'Of course I did. And, furthermore, I turned it down. The South is not my country. And I will not be anyone's vassal. So I told her where she could put her patronage. She seemed quite surprised.'

There's hope for the old girl yet, I think, and feel considerably more cheerful.

'I really should go back soon,' says Albanna.

'You have a busy schedule, I presume. They'll be getting full value out of you.'

'No one ever bothers to fill me in on the arrangements,' she says, with a touch of petulance, 'but I think I am being taken to some military encampment for afternoon tea with the warriors' wives.'

'We couldn't let you miss that.'

'Of course not. There will probably be smoked salmon sandwiches.'

'If it wouldn't cramp your style, perhaps I could go with you. I think I'd find it most enlightening.'

She looks doubtful. 'They'd notice. I'm sure it wouldn't be allowed.'

'Just trust me,' I reply. 'I think I'd look quite fetching in a pair of dark glasses and one of those undercover agent raincoats.'

Albanna's minders are so relieved to see her strolling down the Royal Mile that they do not even notice the secret policewoman guiding her gently by the elbow. I flash my identity card (a lot easier to conjure up than one of those bits of plastic for the money-machines) and take my place within the official convoy.

The visit to the Officers' Wives is not the most exciting of adventures, but I have my reasons for sticking close to Albanna's side.

Dill, on twin patrol, regales the girls with an unusual treat: ice cream that is ordered from a waitress. An exciting change from home, where cones and sundaes are normally conjured from thin air. At Mr IceCream's Parlour they plunge into a riot of raspberry-sauced and whipped-cream-crested mountains of Mango Cheese-cake Surprise and Coco-Rococo-Toffee, all decorated with spar-klers and the flags of many nations.

The experiment is a great success: gorged to the point of exhaustion, they behave impeccably on the bus, accept baths with good grace, play quietly and with no altercations until bedtime, and even volunteer to brush their teeth.

Dill feels all this is too good to be true. She is right. While the twins debate the relative merits of *Thomas the Land Rover* and *Pat the Privatized Postman* for their bedtime story, someone pounds on the front door. On the threshold stands a slim woman with an even slimmer briefcase, and her male companion, a V-shaped hulk. A dark-blue van stands at the kerbside, with its motor running.

'North British Social Adjustment Consultants,' announces the woman, flashing an ID card.

'I have all the insurance I need, thank you,' says Dill, closing the door.

Before it reaches the jamb, Hulk inserts a foot in it.

'We may come in,' says his partner, who clearly outranks him.

'What?'

'We may, can, are legally authorized to, whatever you like, enter these premises. Under Clause 86, Subsection 33, of the Sexual Normality Act. I am obliged to tell you that you are hereby charged with corrupting minors by the maintenance of a Pretended Family Relationship.' She draws a pocket-sized computer from her butter-soft leather briefcase and punches in some numbers. 'Two, female. Aged three years and six months. We are removing them for their own protection.'

Dill's petit-bourgeois upbringing goes down the pipe. 'Like fuck you are,' she bellows, in fishwifely manner. 'Says who?'

'It's the law, I'm afraid.'

'You can't have them.'

'Come now, dear, you're a professional. Dentist, is it? I'll just check. Oh, terribly sorry, doctor. You wouldn't want to be struck off the register, would you, for interfering with a government contractor carrying out its legitimate business? Or charged with yet another offence against Public Order? It could mean a longer, much nastier sentence, the second time around. We know all about you, you see. So I must ask you to hand over the minors at once.'

'Piss off. And take Frankenstein's monster with you!'

His vast hands clench into fists. Dill sees the glint of a knuckle-duster – or maybe just his wedding ring. He pushes past her, while his power-dressed lady sidekick pins Dill to the wall. He reappears quickly – the bijou maisonette takes little time to search – with a squirming twin tucked under each arm.

To the fascination of her neighbours, peering out from behind the rubber plants in their bay windows, Dill runs after the van, screaming and cursing. Then she staggers back to the house, just in time to catch the telephone before it stops ringing. It's me.

'Gwhyldis, oh my goddess, I . . .'

'Did I interrupt bathtime? Never mind, they won't drown. I have only a few seconds. Just to say I won't be back until tomorrow. Can't explain now. Just be sure to keep tomorrow evening free . . .'

'Wait, they've . . .'

'Can't stay chatting. Someone's coming. Hold the fort and love to the wee ones. Byee.'

'You needn't stay around on my account,' announces Albanna, marching into the room as I put down the telephone. She seems decidedly twitchy. 'You don't want that interesting girlfriend of yours getting jealous, do you?'

'Don't flatter yourself.'

'When things come to a head, I'm sure you'll be among the first to know. And I trust I can count on you to turn up if there is any serious trouble.'

'It's time we made our first move.'

'As I've told you before, leave the strategy to me. Besides, nothing is going to happen tonight.'

'Why not?'

'Because I have what is known, in contemporary parlance, as a dinner date.'

'A dinner date? With whom?'

'With a man. Don't be shocked.'

'Nothing you do has been able to shock me for at least fifteen hundred years. Who's the lucky boy?'

'The Secretary of State for Style has invited me to a discreet but luxurious establishment celebrated for its fine wine list and five-star cuisine.'

'What for? Another ceremonial ribbon-cutting?'

'Strictly off-duty. And top-secret. He's booked a private dining-room for a little *tête-à-tête*.'

'Could he be trying to seduce you?'

'Hardly likely. Although he's a handsome devil, right enough. I wonder if he has a sister?'

She may not want me around for this beanfeast, but I am there in spirit, with ears perked up.

Over the champagne and canapés, the Secretary puts her at ease with talk of the weather. While savouring the fresh foie gras, he listens raptly to Albanna's account of her own military and diplomatic successes. Spooning the crayfish consommé, he pays courtly compliments on her achievements. Between mouthfuls of lobster *millefeuille*, he earnestly solicits her views on a wide range of pressing political and economic issues. With the Calvados sorbet, he praises her sagacity. Sipping the Château Latour, and savouring the grouse, he twinkles and tells racy stories, including one at the PM's expense. With the arrival of the cheeseboard, his voice grows low and his manner confidential. By the last lick of *marquise au chocolat*, Albanna leans towards him, expectant and attentive. Over coffee and petits fours, he sketches out a little hypothetical plan for a quiet *coup d'état*. By the second glass of Armagnac, the pact is made.

Dill's night is less delightful. She paces the cramped sitting-room, trying and then abandoning every trick she has ever learned for staying professionally cool in a crisis. Then, in some undusted attic of her brain, a light flicks on.

In this small and introspective city, gossip rides the bracing southwesterlies. Old acquaintances, living less than a mile away, may be successfully avoided for ten years or more, but any news about them travels at the speed of sound. Dill remembers a recent titbit about a certain friend from student days who has finally Sold Out.

'Guess who's just become Medical Officer for the North British Social Adjustment Consultancy . . .'

'Never!'

'Danny Dalziel??? You're joking!'

Ah yes, Danny Dalziel. Who would have thought it? The world has turned upside down. The moving force in Scalpel Rouge. One-time spokesperson of COMA – the Collective of Medical Activists. Guardian of the guttering flame of medical student radicalism. Will the last fighter to leave the barricades please switch out the lights? Dill remembers those days well – splinter groups and schisms in smoke-filled bedsits, arguments over the wording of leaflets, endless cups of ideologically acceptable coffee. Only the need to study for Finals stopped the revolutionary juggernaut in its tracks.

But Dill is in no mood for meanderings down memory lane. She spends the night waking up everyone she can think of who might know his present, ex-directory home number. Succeeding only in annoying or puzzling a large selection of acquaintances and former friends who haven't thought about Danny in fifteen years, she is forced to wait until the working day begins. The Social Adjusters, in this instance mercifully, start work early. She strains her ears to catch any background noise of caterwauling twins. Instead, she is regaled with anodyne taped music, until Dr Dalziel's secretary announces that he is in a staff meeting until half-past ten. Dill's fingernails are down to nubs, her carpet is worn out with pacing, until she reaches him.

'Marion Dillon – Dill! Of course I remember you! Darling! Where have you been all these years? What have you been doing?'

This is all for the sake of diplomacy. There is not a medic in Edinburgh who does not know about Dr Dillon's window-smashing and subsequent sentence.

'We must get together . . .'

'Well, that's why I'm ringing, actually.'

He offers lunch, some time next week. She counters with a proposal for coffee in half an hour.

To her amazement, he agrees.

In a stone-flagged basement coffee house on the edge of the New Town, Dr Danny Dalziel sits enthroned in a woven-backed Orkney chair, applying home-made rhubarb jam to a treacle scone.

'You haven't changed a bit,' lies Dill. The Trotskyist cheekbones are now covered with a neat red beard, the pugnacious flying picketer's chin has doubled, the tiny gold stud is gone from the earlobe, and the slogan-painted T-shirt has given way to a discreetly expensive business suit.

'You know I have. But let's catch up on personal news later. I've ordered you a pot of Lapsang Souchong. Still your favourite? Good. Nice to see that some things don't change in this cosmic bubble bath of perpetual flux and illusion . . .'

'What?'

'Didn't you know? I've become a Buddhist.'

'Don't I remember you saying something about religion being the Valium of the petty bourgeoisie?'

'I was a pretentious stripling, wasn't I? Anyway, to business. I assume you have some urgent ulterior motive for renewing auld acquaintance . . .'

Dill chooses her words with care. She always did have a soft spot for Danny. But now he has joined the forces of evil. Who are, let us not forget, in possession of the twins. A little tightrope-walking may be necessary, not to mention the kissing of arses and eating of dirt. She prepares to compromise herself – left, right and centre.

I honestly believe she has become genuinely fond of the little terrors. I am touched.

'The Social Adjustment Consultancy . . .'

'Don't look at me like that. Every time I run into one of the old comrades we have to go through this group therapy and self-denunciation routine. In spite of the fact that they're all getting filthy rich in their private practices, with little perks like drug company trials on the side. Not to mention all those important medical conventions on tropical islands.'

'This is not a guilt trip, Danny. This is a cry for help. Your outfit has nicked my . . . friend's children.'

His face closes up. 'Battering – and worse – happens in the nicest families. Kids have to be protected. There's nothing even you could call reactionary about that.'

'I suppose you think they have to be protected from contact with parents who aren't your conventional nucleo-hetero mamas and papas.'

He reddens, collapses into himself, can't meet her eye. 'Not another Subsection 33, is it?'

'Got it. The Gestapo came last night. One lady in a designer jacket and the hulk from outer space. Took them away kicking and screaming. You really have signed on with a charming outfit, Dalziel. I'll bet your old freethinking Red Clydeside Daddy would be proud . . .'

(Hold your fire, Dill. You're supposed to be buttering him up.)

'Let's have lunch.'

'What?'

'We've got to talk about this.'

'I suppose you're going to offer me electroconvulsive aversion therapy at bargain prices to straighten me out. Or maybe a few sessions at Orgasms Anonymous to help me come to terms with renouncing this unfortunate perversion.'

He peers out furtively from the basketwork shelter of the Orkney chair, and scans the room for spies.

'Don't be stupid. I'm going to help you get your kids back.'

'Sorry. All right, lunch. But it's only half-past eleven.'

'It will take us a while to get where we're going. The Reception Centre is down in the Borders, and it just happens that I'm due there this afternoon. Hang on a minute, and I'll give my office a buzz, to let them know I won't be back.'

Inevitably, he produces a nifty little phone from his pocket and whispers to it, as if into the ear of a lover.

Dr Dalziel's company car is just what Dill expected, all luxury and leather. As Danny unlocks the door, he looks faintly embarrassed. They roar up the Mound, and head south. All the lights in the city turn green for their passage: Dill scents a good omen, and wonders if somewhere, somehow, I am poised to intervene. Only when the southern suburbs have given way to abandoned coal-mines and fields of grazing sheep does Danny switch off the quadraphonic sound system, halfway through a silvery saxophone solo, and begin to speak.

'Don't think I'm not aware of the contradictions . . .'

If the price of recovering the twins is a drive through the Borders, while the former firebrand of Scalpel Rouge justifies himself to an old fellow-comrade, Dill is willing to pay it. But the prospect of lunch makes her queasy. She can think of nothing but what I will do to her if she can't get the twins back. Turn her into a flock of ravens? Curse her with the Pictish Pox? Or, worst of all, disappear from her life and her bed forever?

So she listens.

He says, for a start, he's only a minor cog in the organization. Resident medic for the Reception Centre and regional hostels. The higher mandarins of the Company make the policy, do the bidding of the government, and run the show without consulting him. He's there only to give the jabs and treat the chickenpox. A mere technician.

Dill bites her tongue to avoid any remarks about people who just follow orders.

'Besides, if I weren't here, who knows what sort of fascist pig they'd have as their Medical Officer?'

He glances at Dill, who is staring straight ahead.

'You think I'm being defensive, don't you? Well, don't you?'

'Well, if you must know . . .'

'Okay, I admit it. I hate the bloody job.'

'So why'd you take it?'

'Had to do something.'

'Oh, come now – with the possible exception of my own well-publicized case, there are very few doctors on the breadline. What made you so unemployable?'

'I was about to be struck off.'

'For what? Chronic socialist tendencies?'

He turns into the tree-lined drive of a country house hotel. Dill hopes he is not expecting her to buy lunch, in exchange for springing the captives.

'Fell madly in love with a patient.'

'Oh, dear me. Well, you're not the first one. Why didn't you just get her to change her doctor?'

'Too late. We were caught . . . in a clinch. By one of my colleagues in the practice.'

'That wasn't clever.'

'And besides . . . it wasn't a she.'

'Danny!'

'We do have a lot to catch up on.'

For the first time in eighteen hours, Dill feels hungry. She realizes that no food has passed her lips since her scoop of Passion Fruit and Papaya Sorbet at Mr IceCream's yesterday afternoon. She remembers the sight of the twins, up to the ears in whipped cream, and feels her lower lip start to tremble.

Danny notices, and slaps her on the back.

'Darling, leave it to me. You'll have your urchins back sooner than you thought possible. So just settle down and enjoy the world's best wild mushroom soufflé. And it's my treat, by the way, so I can bend your ear about my wonderful boyfriend.'

'Don't look now,' whispers Albanna, through a mouthful of smoked salmon sandwich, 'but I think those are Romans.'

We are not the only guests of the Officers' Wives. A coachload of creaseproof ladies from a nuclear submarine base have come to meet the Ancient Monument in the flesh.

'How do you know?'

'Someone pointed out one of their fortresses when we were up North the other day. They don't speak Latin any more, they come from west instead of east, but otherwise they haven't changed much. Still obsessed with interfering in other people's private business, and fond of eagles. The PM pays them protection money, you know. What a comedown. I remember the days when they paid me.'

'That wasn't protection money, that was a bribe.'

She gives me one of her warning looks. 'I don't pay you to rewrite history.'

Come to think of it, it's been some time since she's paid me at all. Even without interest, my salary arrears now amount to a fairly spectacular sum.

But before I can take her up on this fascinating subject, a bevy of smartly dressed Roman matrons, in drip-dry two-piece togas, bear down on us.

'They're agog to meet me,' whispers Albanna. 'Apparently they have an absolute fixation with British Royalty.'

As the ladies surround us, Albanna's official minder homes in. He is too busy keeping his charge's foot out of the government's mouth to pay attention to the new undercover policewoman who stands at her side. And, boys being boys, he never sees the faint outlines of a tattoo that are beginning to show beneath my hastily applied Sheer Allure foundation make-up.

Nor do the Romans take much notice. They are bent on paying homage.

'Gee, Your Highness, we're so excited to meet you. Absolutely thrilled. You see, back home, we don't have any ancient history of our own. Well, I guess we used to, but it got run over.'

'Just nod and smile, dear,' whispers the Minder, through the corner of his mouth. 'And have a few more of these rather good sandwiches. There's fruitcake coming next.'

Down in her London bunker, the PM has become irritated by some of the reports emanating from the northern provinces. The armchair rebels, tartan lefties and other wild-eyed fanatics have stopped quarrelling with each other just long enough to notice that the Celtic Queen is once more in their midst. Scattered dissidents, limping from the self-inflicted bullet wounds in their feet, are coming out of their burrows.

The fact that Albanna is corralled safely away from close contact with these renegades does not dampen their enthusiasm. Bumper stickers shout at each other on the bypasses and roundabouts, placards utter rallying cries from the windows of city tenements, T-shirts display the lady's famous features above a selection of short, pugnacious slogans. All these are on sale, illegally but openly, on the stalls and barrows of the Souk. And one perspicacious entre-preneur (Dill's old friend Shona, as it happens) has carved out a lucrative niche in the marketplace by offering Hygienic Tattoos in a selection of authentic Celtic patterns. Such outpourings are not what the PM had in mind when she sent the pint-sized barbarian north to show the flag.

In other ages, rulers would have summoned a soothsayer to

analyse the flight patterns of migrating geese, ventured into mountain caves to ask a sibyl's guidance, sacrificed a slave to see which way the blood flowed, then made their plans accordingly. These options are, unfortunately, closed, due to the shortage of suitably qualified professionals (the only one around is yours truly, and I don't work freelance). Instead, the PM is forced to consult (though not always give credence to) opinion polls, secret memoranda, and the market research reports of her streetwise image-makers. These last have done for her what they did for a certain brand of Japanese whisky, several controversial property developments, an automotive white elephant, and the entire Swiss pharmaceutical industry.

In the course of her rise to power, these consultants have reshaped her hair and her profile, altered the timbre of her voice, tinkered with her accent, rechoreographed her body language and transformed her wardrobe. The Creative Department that came up with the prizewinning Glen Shogun Whisky label is also responsible for her script at Question Time.

Founder and former director of the company (now safely lodged in his wife's name) is the Secretary of State for Style. The PM picks up the telephone, tracks him down in Scotland (he is on the job running the Albanna cavalcade) and commands him: 'Dump the Tattooed Lady.'

At first, he demurs. Things, he protests, are going swimmingly up here. The tide is turning. Privately, his heart sinks – the directive, for his staff, will be the equivalent of demolishing a newly built office block, girder by hard-won girder, brick by painstaking brick.

'Stop snivelling.'

So he pulls his expensive socks up and gets on with the job. He does, after all, have an advantage over his fellow-ministers. When his colleagues wish to eradicate opposition or expunge some unpalatable fact, they are forced to cut off funds, devise restrictive legislation, issue injunctions, or otherwise rewrite the rules in the middle of the game. But the Secretary of State for Style has more elegant weapons in his arsenal. Media barons can be lunched, reliable columnists primed and flattered. The way to wipe out subversion is to let the opinion-sculptors yawn and call it boring. He is convinced that if a few important Czarist fashion designers had announced that Red was definitely last year's colour, the Bolshevik Revolution would never have happened.

He has done it with socialism, feminism, gay liberation, anti-racism, liberalism and other public inconveniences, and now he is going to do it with that hairy-legged Celt.

The Reception Centre, set in its own grounds, is the ex-country mansion of some Victorian merchant, all turrets, crow-stepped gables and other Scottish baronial frills. Matron stands in the oak-panelled entrance hall, her face striped blue and orange by the filtered light of stained-glass windows. Danny introduces Dill as a colleague, recently returned from abroad, with an interest in the work of the Social Adjustment Consultancy. He is sure that Matron will not object to an unscheduled visitor, since her Reception Centre – unlike some we won't mention – is always in apple-pie order. Matron, in a cut-price version of the Prime Ministerial hairdo, graciously offers to take Dill on a tour of the premises while Dr Dalziel has a look at two recovering mumps, one chesty cough, and a twisted ankle. 'And that little Fraser, who I am quite sure is crying wolf again. I told him you'd sort him out once and for all with some nasty-tasting medicine and a needle this big in his bottom. I hope you'll oblige.'

'Now then,' purrs Dill's guide, 'let me show you our wee home-away-from-home. We're a very happy, busy place, as you'll no doubt be able to tell from all the noise.'

The rambling old villa echoes with a cacophony of childish voices, teacherly shouts, thumps, poundings, crying babies, tele-visions turned up loud and a distant record-player, all competing.

'This is the day room for the over-eight girls. In you come!'

Ten or fifteen girls sit in a ring on the polished floor, clutching pieces of shiny white fabric and snippets of lace. A woman stands in the centre of the circle, holding up a scrap of cloth and demonstrating a simple stitch.

'Now it has to be a row of four, exactly like that, or it's no use, and I'll have to tear them up and make you start all over again . . . Oh, hello, Matron!'

'Hello, dears. We have a visitor today. She's come to see your sewing circle. And what are we making this afternoon?'

Most of the girls stare, open-mouthed, at the newcomers. A few glower. One tongue, surreptitiously, darts out and in again. Two or three raise their hands high in the air, squirming with excitement.

'Lovely bridal gowns for dollies, Miss,' they chant in perfect unison.

Just behind the circle Dill sees a mountain of bulging polythene sacks, spilling out bolts of the same white cloth and coils of lace ribbon.

'Is that all for bridal gowns?' she asks.

'When we're at full strength, we produce three gross a week,' beams Matron, then turns back to her charges. 'Now, are we sure our hands are perfectly spotless, girls? We don't want a repeat of last week's misfortunes, do we?'

As they scrutinize their fingers, she ushers me out. 'That's all for the Miss TeenDream Dolls contract. They're ever so demanding about quality control. But it's quite a coup for our little establishment. Now, let's see what the over-eight laddies are up to . . .'

The over-eight laddies are attaching thick soles to brown leather Army boots, banging their hammers in time to the martial music that blares from two tall speakers. Matron greets them, and their instructor, with a jaunty military salute, spins smartly on her heel, and marches us out again.

'Just a wee joke of ours. That's a Ministry of Defence job they're on. We're very proud. Now if you come upstairs I'll show you something absolutely marvellous . . .'

She sprints up the oak-panelled staircase, waits patiently while Dill follows at a slower pace, and halts, finger to her lips, at a pair of handsomely carved double doors.

'We'll just keek in,' she whispers, 'in case they're in the middle of a shot . . .'

Tall black screens, just inside the doorway, block the entire room from view.

'Go on,' she urges, 'take a look. You'll be all right if you stand just there, and look round . . .'

Behind the screens, on the polished floor of a stately drawing-room with blacked-out windows, stand thirty or forty children of assorted sizes and ages. They are all wearing canary-yellow tracksuits, emblazoned with the word HEALTHY in bright-green letters.

In the second-to-last row, Dill sees the twins. She stifles the impulse to grab the pair and run. She would, in any case, have to climb over an entire camera crew to reach them. The twins, of course, do not see her: they are dazzled by the banks of hot bright lights and gaze, with a mixture of terror and fascination, upon the autocratic little man in tight blue jeans who stands at one end of the room, fumbling with a clipboard. He seems to have forgotten the children's existence, and is swearing in stage whispers at a colleague in a rumpled suit. But his youthful performers soon remind him of their presence: someone wails about needing the toilet, several start fidgeting, and three or four scuffles break out in the ranks.

He puts two fingers to his lips and restores order with an ear-splitting whistle.

'Right! Now we're going to go through the whole routine again, and this time I want you all to keep to the beat. Those who can do the steps do them, the rest of youse just bounce up and down in time to the music. But either way, I want you smiling, you wee buggers. Let's see some big, wide, cheesy grins. I want some twinkle, damn it. And if I don't get twinkle this time, we're gonna do it again and again and again and again . . . or you'll no get your juice nor your tea nor your bedtime milk and bikkies. Because I'm fully prepared to stay here all night long. Do you hear me . . . ? . . . Right . . . And when you see me wave my arms, begin . . . On the count of three . . . Cue Music!'

Someone switches on a tape and a perky chorus of prerecorded professional juveniles belts out:

'Dancing feet! I've got those dancing feet!

Cos Healthy Pops is what I eat!'

The director gives the signal and the tracksuits begin moving to the music, some merely hopping up and down, others – the twins included – executing a sequence of simple tap-dance steps: *tappy-tappy-tap-tap, tappy-tappy-tap-tap* . . .

Matron, finger to her lips, tugs at Dill's sleeve and draws her away, pausing to shut the double doors with studious gentleness.

'Aren't they a scream?' She looks at her watch. 'Well, just time for a quick cuppy. Wasn't that gorgeous?'

Dill is whisked into an adjoining staff room, where the music and the tap-dancing are clearly audible through the wall.

'Now that', Matron announces over the custard creams, 'is our real little earner. I don't know how well up you are on show business, but let me tell you that the cost of doing that routine with professional child actors would be absolutely astronomical. We negotiate a group rate, which saves the advertising agency a bomb but brings us in a very respectable sum. And that director is just marvellous the way he works with the wee ones. We're very lucky. All the Consultancy's homes show a profit, but ours always comes top of the League. Not even Glasgow can touch us.'

'I'm . . . fascinated.'

'Good. Well, no rest for the weary. I'd better drink up. But you take your time, dear. Put your feet up, if you like. I always do, when I get the chance. Now, do you think you can find your own way back downstairs when you're ready? I've got to tiptoe in next door the minute the music stops and pull out a couple of new arrivals to have their medicals. And, oh dearie me, that director will give me laldy. He says that shifting the bairns between takes plays hell with his continuity. But it can't be helped. Mustn't keep Doctor waiting.'

As Matron inserts herself on to the film set, Dill rushes back downstairs to the room marked Surgery. Danny hustles her behind a screen. Twinly shrieks of recognition would not be helpful.

'Here we are,' sings Matron, steering in the twins, with a hand on the back of each neck. 'Did your colleague find you?'

'Nipped out to the car for a moment. Wanted something out of her briefcase – some offprint from an American journal. She thought you might find it interesting. Now,' he smiles down at the twins, who are looking at him through narrowed, suspicious eyes, 'what have we here? A lovely matched pair . . .' He reaches out, ruffles their hair, then contemplates his upturned palms.

'Wait a minute . . .'

Matron begins to lift off one yellow sweatshirt. 'We'll just pop off your little tracksuits, dears, and . . .'

'No,' says Danny, restraining her. 'Hang on. Would you bring them over to the light for a minute?' He switches on an Anglepoise, swirls it towards the top of one twin's head, parts the hair and peers closely at the scalp. 'Good God! That's worrying. Now the other one, please, Matron. Oh my. Oh dear me. That's one for the textbooks. Very nasty . . .'

'What is it, Doctor?'

'How extraordinary! And this far north!'

'What IS it?' Matron grows tetchy. If all is not well in her little empire, she wants to know. Now.

'*Sapphis Platonica* – of all things . . .'

'Well?'

'Very rare. Just pray we're not in for a Scottish epidemic . . .'

'Doctor! I would like to know what's going on!'

'Oh, sorry, Matron. Just a bit of a shock to see it for myself, that's all. A very exotic strain of head lice. And very virulent. With some fascinating side-effects. Usually found in the Mediterranean. Must be the run of unseasonably mild weather, bringing it up this far. Or all those package holidays.'

'What sort of side-effects?'

'Well, serious infestations – and they usually are serious – seem to be associated with a temporary loss of nocturnal bladder control . . .'

'I don't like the sound of that one bit. Is it easily spread?'

'Like wildfire, I'm afraid.'

'What are we to do?'

'Well, first of all we'll get this pair well away from here. Like as not they're the source of infection. Then, you'd better give every-body – and I mean everybody, staff included – a very thorough headwash with a disinfectant shampoo. Then put rubber sheets on all the beds, and hope for the best.'

She begins to babble about staff costs, overtime, the laundry budget and disrupted routine until Danny silences her with a peremptory bark.

'Matron! There is no need to panic. If these two just came in last night, there's a good chance that the worst can be avoided. As long as we act promptly.'

'But the film people, upstairs . . .'

'Tell them it's a medical emergency. In the meantime, I'll get these two into isolation. There's a new hush-hush quarantine unit opened up in the Highlands. I'll run our two cases up there this afternoon.'

'How much will it . . . ?'

'No, don't worry about the cost. We can pay for it out of my departmental budget instead of yours. Just mark this pair Discharged. I'll sort out the rest of the paperwork at my end, and get them sorted out in another hostel once the bugs are gone. But best keep the whole thing confidential. We don't want to start a panic, and lose our reputation as Most Hygienic Reception Centre in the Group, do we? Now, then. Do they have any gear?'

'No, they just came in their nightclothes.'

'Good. Burn them. And any towels and bedding too. And don't forget the shampoos all round, for goodness' sake. I'll be in touch.'

Matron dashes out to nip the crisis in the bud.

I emerge from behind the screen, finger to lips. The twins, finding all this immensely funny, put their fingers to their lips as well. All four of us scuttle out, pile into Danny's company car, and head for Morningside, with New Orleans jazz blaring out from all four speakers.

'Anybody home?' I certainly can choose my moment.

I stroll into the kitchen, to find Dill heating up some soup for the twinlets' supper.

'Sorry to be so late. Whenever that woman is involved, things always take twice as long as they're meant to.' I turn to the twins who are occupying the rest of the pocket-handkerchief kitchen.

'Well, hello, girls. I see we've been taken shopping for new tracksuits. But my goodness, Dill, what a peculiar colour. Never mind. I assume you've both been good as gold while I've been gone.'

'*Tappy-tappy-tap-tap, tappy-tappy-tap-tap,*' is the twosome's only reply.

Dill recounts the saga of the twins' abduction and subsequent rescue. 'I suppose you think it's all my fault,' she says, with a touch of belligerence. 'Letting those Social Adjustment bastards get a foot in the door.'

But I offer nothing but sympathy for her plight and praise for her solution. What else was she to do – pour boiling lead upon the raiders from the roof?

'I am impressed,' I announce, 'and deeply, deeply touched. You obviously have better maternal instincts than you suspected. Not to mention a sneaking fondness for my terrible twins. So how about giving up your stall in the Souk and coming home to be a mother to our darling little girls?'

'Piss off.'

Humourless feminist.

The twins entertain us with their tap-dance routine – eleven times. The twelfth performance is mercifully interrupted by a telephone call from Danny Dalziel. He thought Dill might like to know that the Social Adjusters' computer records have been subjected to a little readjustment of their own. We should have no further cause for worry.

'We may need supernatural means to tire them out tonight,' says Dill. 'They're high as kites.'

'I'll see what I can do. It had better be early to bed and early to rise for all of us, because tomorrow night we may not get any sleep at all. With your permission, of course. I have an unmissable treat in store.'

Dill looks hopeful, gives me a lustful wink.

'Alas, not yet. This particular agenda involves some good, clean family entertainment. The Winter Solstice celebrations on Arthur's Seat.'

After the girls are bathed and bedded, I give Dill a partial account of my adventures: the afternoon with the military matrons, followed by a cocktail reception with a party of company directors. Their interest in Albanna was limited; they gave her the same perfunctory once-over they might bestow on a factory site in a region without development grants, and turned away – as swiftly as good manners allow – to plot hostile takeovers of each other's corporations.

Nevertheless, I decide to leave out the details of Albanna's little dinner date. Far safer to wait a while and see how things pan out. 'Spent it massaging Madam's ego,' I say, when Dill asks about the evening. 'Nobody's sung her praises enough lately. I had to step into the breach or there'd have been tears before bedtime.'

CHAPTER SIX

I AM NOT THE ONLY one who knows how to economize on the truth. The Secretary of State for Style proves himself a master of the art. At the moment, he and the Colonial Governor sprawl upon Regency sofas in an inner sanctum at the Debriefing Centre. Ties undone and armpits itching, they recover from the rigours of the day.

'Message from on high, dear boy. The PM's new game-plan. Albanna gets the old heave-ho. Boss wants her out of the limelight. Permanently. And soon.'

'Not before time. I didn't think this comedy would run and run. And it doesn't seem to have done much for us in the Opinion Polls.' He yawns and stretches. 'Squiring the old girl around the high spots is all very well, but I still have a province to run. People yammering about school closures, sky-pilots getting too big for their boots, an ultimatum from the police about the budgets for the Containment Centres, a load of chancers trying it on with compensation claims about that little You-Know-What accident in the Firth of Clyde last year. You name it. Not to mention the water stushie.'

'Sounds like one of your quaint Celtic fairy tales.'

'Don't you laugh. I'm faced with thousands of agitators stirring up hysteria about the contamination in Standard Class tap water. As if they weren't perfectly free to pay the higher charge and opt for Premium Grade. You pay your money and you take your choice, we tell them. But, once again, I cannot drive the message through their skulls.'

'Maybe it's all that lead in their pipes. Lowers the IQ, so they say.'

The Colonial Governor sniffs. 'Just you pray the water companies iron all the kinks out before they launch the scheme down South.'

'Oh, we've already worked out our campaign. They're painting all the Standard Class mains taps and pipework in a spectacularly hideous colour. Any home-owner with a particle of concern about What the Neighbours Think will choose the higher grade. And the aspirational advertising for Premium Grade is a dream: I shouldn't be surprised if it scoops all the industry awards.'

They turn their attention to the next day's agenda.

'If we're easing her out of public view, shouldn't we just fold our tents and cancel the photo opportunities?'

'On the contrary,' says the Secretary. 'The strategy is oversaturation. We're going to bore the public into stupefaction. By the end of the week the very mention of the words Albanna, Celtic, Ancient, Queen and Amazon will send them instantly to sleep. I've reorganized tomorrow's schedule into a blitz of guest appearances at out-of-town DIY superstore openings, Cub Scout prize-givings, old folks' whist drives, and Bonny Baby competitions. Image-wise, the kiss of death.'

'Damn! I suppose the PM will want us to cancel her participation in the druidical Solstice rites on Arthur's Seat. I don't know how I'm going to square that with the Lodge Brothers . . .'

'No problem. I've already checked with Number 10. She says to go ahead, but bar the television crews.'

'Well, the Brethren certainly won't object to that. They feel the whole thing has turned into too much of a publicity circus – what with all those astral projectors and Goddess-worshipping lesbians cluttering up the site.'

'Oh, I wouldn't worry about that this year. She also wants you to impose an official ban on everyone but the Druidicals.'

'This will take a spot of paperwork,' grins the Colonial Governor. 'Not to mention a lot of liaison time with the police – discussing roadblocks and identity checks, and so forth.' He pulls out his pocket-sized computer diary, punches keys and ponders the tiny screen. 'No way to squeeze it all in, I'm afraid. You'd better do tomorrow's escort duty without me. I'm sure you'll enjoy the Bonny Babies.'

'I'll get you for that,' says the Secretary of State for Style.

*

Meanwhile, down in the imperial capital, the curtains of the Prime Ministerial windows are drawn tight against the freezing fog rising up from the Thames. Not even a sliver of light reveals itself to the street below, where the usual gaggle of awed subjects and curious tourists gather beyond the electronic barricades. The PM is in conference with her innermost circle of advisers, a body so secret that not even the official Cabinet is privy to its deliberations.

Its members are as obscure as they are powerful: not one face among them would be recognized in the unlikely event that its owner should ever mingle with the crowds. They are private citizens: their attendance upon the PM is unsalaried, and unrecorded. When not providing support and counsel, they collect multinational corporations, Monets and Ming vases. They own media barons as other men own Irish setters (keeping them on the same length of leash). You will not find them in airports with the lesser business nobility, waiting for their flights in softly lit executive lounges: they have their own aircraft, and the planes wait for them.

Although they are sworn blood brothers within the Prime Ministerial cabal, there is little love – and no trust – lost between them. But they are married to each other's former wives, sit together in boardrooms all over the financial world, and have survived cruises on each other's pleasure-boats without tragic mishaps. In short, they enjoy a fruitful working relationship.

'But who gets custody of the body? All the drug companies are bidding.'

'So are the cosmetics firms. Rejuvenation creams now account for a larger share of the GNP than petrochemicals.'

'Hang on, old chap,' interposes someone whose country mansion, Chelsea flat and Caribbean retreat all float on a slick of South-East Asian oil, 'I think you're misreading the figures.'

'Absolutely not. You'll find the data in the latest circular from the Statistical Manipulation Commission.'

The PM claps her hands for silence. 'We're straying from the point!'

'Quite right, ma'am. As it happens, my old college has a very interesting research proposal . . .'

'Hands off. So does mine.'

'Hold on a minute, gentlemen. We must first deal with a small technical problem. Are we quite sure it will be possible to . . . dispatch her? Presumably, in technical terms, she's already dead.'

'We shall do some on-the-spot research. I have ordered up a selection of classic zombie films from the archives. I daresay their scriptwriters long ago came up with the appropriate solutions – just as they did for space travel, laser weapons and the rest.'

At the touch of a button, heavy black shutters seal off the thickly curtained windows. A wall parts to expose a screen.

'When you're ready,' murmurs the PM into an intercom. 'Choc-ice, anyone?'

They've tried, over time, to ban it or bury it, or disguise it as a festival of frenzied last-minute shopping; they've rewritten the script, fiddled with the calendar, and introduced a whole new cast of characters. I have no objection to those who wish to treat it as a birthday party for some perfectly harmless little boy from Palestine, and the animal sacrifices are certainly nothing new. (But why a turkey? Whose tribal totem is that?)

In accordance with their ancient rite (going back at least three generations) the Druids prepare to conduct their semi-annual Solstice rites on Arthur's Seat. This is the members' privilege; they have just as much right and reason to be there as Aquarian tourists tracking ley lines, or local joggers making their bid for eternal youth. But if Mr Melville, Lord Corbiestane, the Earl of Ballingry and the rest of the boys' club claim that the hill belongs to them alone, don't blame me if I'm not the only party that feels slightly miffed.

Nor will the news please Albanna, who believes, after all, that this unfortunately misnamed lump of rock is her personal domain, and would like to extract rent and tribute from all who set foot on it.

Strangely enough, word gets around.

Normally, the December ceremonies are sparsely attended. A midnight bonfire in balmy June is one thing; a huddled congregation greeting the dawn in the frost of December is quite another. But the one time the Druids try to make this a private party, everybody wants to come.

*

'If they aren't letting anybody up there but Lodge members,' Dill demands, 'how are we going to get on to Arthur's Seat?'

'Hand me those bed-sheets,' I reply, 'and the sewing scissors. We're about to join the Druids.'

'What about the twins?'

'They'll be safe. But I promised them they won't miss out on the fun.'

Albanna stands with her arms folded, watching the druidical caperings. Absorbed in their rites, they have forgotten her existence – except for the Colonial Governor, who keeps shooting sidelong glances to make sure she hasn't bolted from her minders.

Her lips are pursed, her brows furrowed.

At the solemn moment of sunrise, when the first slender shafts of winter light illuminate the waters of the Firth of Forth, and the Brethren of the Lodge link white-sleeved arms to salute the holiest of Dawns, she clears her throat, very loudly.

'Cow dung,' she announces. 'Goat's farts. And ox piss.'

Her hosts, their trances broken, look at her with some annoyance.

'This ceremony, gentlemen, is a travesty. I'm surprised the sun is willing to come out at all, given the way you've bungled it. I'm only thankful Her Holiness the Archpriestess Gwhyldis isn't here to see this. There'd be no holding her back. She'd bang some heads together.'

But of course I am here, along with Dill, disguised in vestments plundered from the linen cupboard in Morningside. Albanna sees us, but gives no sign.

She continues her attack: 'I don't suppose you've even prepared a sacrifice.'

Druidical irritation is now coupled with puzzlement.

'Liberals can say what they like, but this just proves it. There is no place for the male sex in religion. You lack the wit, the passion and the attention to detail. And I can't think what the goddesses will make of all this mumbo jumbo. I'm afraid you have only yourselves to blame if this year's crops fail.'

She looks about her. 'What about him?' she demands, pointing to the Earl of Ballingry. 'With that corn-coloured hair. A perfect little morsel for the Grain Mother. Truss him up and we'll have his cinders fertilizing the earth in no time.'

She strides up, looks him in the eye.

'Are you a virgin?'

He splutters.

'I thought not. Pity. It was too good to be true. Well, you've missed your chance for glory, my friend.'

There is a general consensus among the senior Druids – the Master of the Mistletoe, the Guardian of the Sacred Grove, the Catering Chairman and the Membership Secretary – that the rite should be brought swiftly to its conclusion. The Lodge members, moreover, are eager to repair to their headquarters for the final phase of the ceremony: restorative brandies, in generous measure, to bring the circulation back to cold-nipped extremities. Albanna is unlikely to be invited.

The Colonial Governor feels he may have lost some credibility with the Brethren. The Amazon's attendance has not been a success. He directs her minders to bundle her back to base; he'll follow on later. He cannot afford to miss the brandy session at the Lodge, lest rival factions take the chance to murmur behind his back. For this is the place where careers, like business deals and fat public contracts, are made and broken.

But no one is going anywhere.

'There seems to be a spot of trouble down the hill,' reports the Secretary. 'Some sort of hippy convoy. The police think you ought to have a look for yourself.'

The Colonial Governor curses through his teeth. 'What do they need me for? They know their orders. Nobody gets in except Lodge members with security passes.'

'That's the trouble. They all seem to have one. And there are thousands of them.'

'Okay, I admit it,' I say to Dill, 'I didn't spend the whole of yesterday watching Albanna cutting ribbons at new supermarkets.

There were jobs to do, arrangements to be made, plots to watch hatching.'

One has to seize the moment. A solstice always finds me at the height of my powers.

'And now, my darling, if you don't mind,' I say to Dill, 'I have a little assignment for you. The trouble is, you may have to work with some people you don't really like very much.'

I explain the plan. Dill splutters. She doesn't seem very impressed. 'Talk about getting into bed with the enemy!' she snarls.

'Be pragmatic. Take the long view . . .'

She is unconvinced – indeed, appalled – by the arrangements when I spell them out to her. I pull rank, remind her I have a trick or two up my sleeve, vow that everything will work out for the best in the end, and promise her untold delights: they include, in addition to some treats that are for nobody else's ears, a commitment to do all the laundry and washing up until some time in the next century.

Not persuasive enough. Then comes my trump card. 'Well, Doctor, do you have any better ideas?'

Reluctantly, she agrees to play it my way.

'This will all end in tears,' she warns.

'Ah yes, but whose?' I counter.

She stomps off down the hill, then suddenly stops in her tracks.

'Better hurry,' I shout after her. 'The timing's tight.'

At first I think she has changed her mind once more, and gone on strike. Then I realize she is transfixed by something at the bottom of the slope.

'Who are all those people?' she asks, pointing down towards the road that skirts Dunsapie Loch.

'Oh, them? How silly of me. I completely forgot; you've never been introduced. Come and meet the family before you go.'

I suppose, if you're not used to them, a large army of tattooed Amazons in full battledress could be a daunting sight. Dill says it's the smell that hits you first. They're really quite a reasonable bunch, although they don't like to be kept waiting. So the police were at something of a loss to deal with them when they grew tired of queueing up, as originally instructed, to show their druidical membership cards to the officers in charge.

The situation grows even more delicate when our cavalry comes up. I suppose every riding stable in the Lothians will be wondering what happened to its horses; even so, there aren't nearly enough to go round. But where we come from, you don't survive for long if you aren't good at making do. So I am hardly surprised when two of our commanders arrive in a borrowed Rolls-Royce. The vehicle is far less manoeuvrable than their customary wicker war chariots: I'm sure they never actually intended to crash straight through those police barriers.

The police, predictably, call for reinforcements. There are some important people being taken hostage up there on the hill: individuals indispensable to the National Interest. Not only the Colonial Governor, but Lord Corbiestane, the Earl of Ballingry and other worthies who, conspicuously or quietly, run the show. It would be more than the Chief Constable's job is worth to let harm come to a single hair of their distinguished heads.

But any relief vehicles will have a hard time getting through. Not only is every rockface and slope alive with swarming warriors, but the roads through the park will soon be impassable. Nature herself has come to our aid.

'Look,' says Albanna to the Chief Druid, who squirms in the grip of two hefty Proto-Pictish maidens. She points to the rocky outcrop on the leonine head of Arthur's Seat, where a plume of smoke rises into the sky. Below it, liquid bubbles up from a newly opened crater.

'Now see what you've done,' she chides him. 'The mountain is awake again. That will teach you boys to go meddling with forces you can't control.'

The lava that now bursts forth from the summit smells of leeks, carrots, lentils, barley and a lot of stored-up grievances. It is the soup immemorial of all Scottish grandmothers, and there seems to be an inexhaustible supply.

Just as the demented doctor on the tropical island is about to be overpowered by his own staring zombies run amok, a blade of light slices across the cinema screen.

'Terribly, terribly sorry to interrupt, ma'am . . .'

'I said we were not to be disturbed. This had better be something urgent. Well?'

'Reports of a disaster coming in. From Edinburgh. Something they thought was a dead volcano has just erupted.'

At a word, the screen goes dark and the lights come on again.

'Good God,' murmurs a magnate of the inner circle, 'Arthur's Seat!'

'How dreadful!' the PM intones, in the resonant alto reserved for such occasions. 'Many casualties?'

Could that be a hopeful glint in her eye?

A military aircraft waits to speed the PM to the scene. She heads across the tarmac twice before her actual departure, for the benefit of a late-arriving television news crew. The stride is, as always, purposeful. 'Now, now,' say the high-heeled footsteps, 'brave boys don't cry. Nanny's on her way, and we are going to get to the bottom of this.'

She hopes that this time someone has been sensible enough to separate the truly grateful survivors from the ones who wake to find her at their bedsides and fall into fits of helpless rage.

As her aircraft hits cruising altitude, directly over a derelict industrial estate somewhere in the East Midlands, her Cabinet – or those members who are not unavoidably, and judiciously, detained elsewhere – meets in an extraordinary secret session. The Minister for Patriotism, hotfoot from Scotland with a briefcase full of confidential papers chained to his wrist, chairs the meeting. It will not take long: the agenda is short and very, very sweet.

A dark shadow looms over the land. The Prime Ministerial plane flies over the border.

From her vantage point on the top of Arthur's Seat, Albanna watches the Prime Minister circling like a bat in the lavender light of the winter morning, over the low hills of East Lothian and the shores of Fife.

'Here comes your mistress,' she announces. 'What a pity she missed the ceremony. But never mind, at least she's in time to review my troops.'

The Secretary of State for Style, uncharacteristically, nudges her and winks. Equally uncharacteristically, she winks and nudges back.

The troops, now only a few yards away, bear little resemblance to the soldiers the Secretary knows from Sandhurst. They regale him with a medley of their favourite battle cries.

'Baying for blood,' smiles Albanna. 'Whatever shall we do?'

What we see before us, in the very shadow of the venerable royal palace of Holyrood, is not your standard-issue old lefty demonstration, the sort where dissidents once made comradely speeches, waved handsome banners, met their friends, bought each other's leaflets, and scowled at the splinter groups for lowering the tone, before such activities were banned.

This particular scenario is not covered in any of the training manuals issued for the guardians of the status quo. All the community relations courses, martial arts practice, Outward Bound survival weekends and riot shields in the world could not assist the police in restoring law and order to Arthur's Seat and the surrounding park. And all the Nato joint manoeuvres, regimental dinners and arms dealers in the world could not prepare the Army for an encounter with Albanna's forces.

Modern weapons technology, of which they know nothing, does not impress the Amazons; they do not deign to notice what they cannot comprehend.

Undaunted, they advance to meet the massed forces of State power face to face. And walk straight through them.

Albanna swings into action. We have a small disagreement over a site for the strategy conference with our senior officers. She plumps for the Fortress of the Maidens, for old times' sake; I point out that it is now far too cluttered up with medieval chapels, military museums, souvenir shops and other newfangled distractions.

I come up with an inspired alternative, and point it out to Albanna as we pace back and forth across the top of Arthur's Seat, carefully sidestepping the volcanic ooze.

'Excellent,' she says. 'Spread the word among the general staff. Rendezvous at the site in two hours precisely.'

The good burghers of Edinburgh, hell-bent on Christmas shopping, hardly see the tattooed strangers in Princes Street. A football or rugby crowd, or the tourists at Festival time, clog up the pavements just as badly. Locals are skilled in the art of ignoring their existence. It isn't as if these were people they went to school with. But the bagpiping busker notices, as do the teenaged homeless, shivering in their tents at the foot of the Mound, alongside the National Gallery's classical façade. They realize, sooner than most, that something is up. The daily routine has been disrupted. Here it is, nearly 10 a.m., and no police have arrived to remove them from the picture-postcard scene. And the air, for some reason, smells of soup.

When the Prime Ministerial helicopter touches down in the Meadows, just behind the Royal Infirmary, she is greeted by the Secretary of State for Style, accompanied by a solemn duet of doctors in crisp white coats.

'Terrible thing, this. Just appalling,' she observes, with a sigh. Yet despite her grave expression, there is an unmistakable spring in her step. Natural disasters are her favourite kind: no fear of awkward outcries about mismanagement or penny-pinching at the expense of public safety.

'Before we inspect the scene of the catastrophe, we should like to have a word with some survivors.'

'Of course, ma'am, at once,' says Dr Daniel Dalziel, with an audible click of the heels.

'But, with all due respect,' interposes his colleague, Dr Marion Dillon, 'I'm afraid we shall have to ask you to leave your – ' she indicates the phalanx of security men ' – associates outside the ward. We cannot subject the victims to the threat of infection.'

'Not even a television news team?' gasps the PM. 'Then what on earth is the point of my coming all the way up here and . . .'

'We understand,' soothes Dr Dalziel. 'And we've made appropriate arrangements. You'll find a pair of representative media persons waiting inside. Both suitably disinfected, of course. But a larger party would pose an unacceptable risk . . .'

'We wouldn't want any harm to come to those innocent bystanders who have suffered so much already, would we?'

'Lead me to them,' commands the PM, reprogramming her body language into Compassion Mode.

A dab hand at disaster visits, the PM is bemused by this one.

For a place that has just received – indeed, must still be receiving – scores of casualties, the ward is oddly silent. No intercoms crackle, no buzzers sound, no monitors bleep. This should not be surprising. If the PM were as Argus-eyed as her minions and devotees like to think, she would have seen the relevant memoranda months ago: the hospital has been closed down since October, and now awaits the property developers who have bought it for a song for conversion into luxury maisonettes and executive penthouse flats.

Yet there is a patient in every bed, sitting bolt upright with arms folded, scrutinizing the illustrious visitor as she seeks out a photogenic victim.

The PM pauses beside the bed of a white-haired old lady, who seems to be smiling bravely. A law-and-order fan if ever she saw one: well worth a caring pat on the hand.

'And how did you come to be in the path of the volcano, dear?' she croons.

The answer, in a lilting Fife accent, is all but incomprehensible. The PM bends low, cups her hand to her hairdo, and says, 'Come again?' There is, after all, a television microphone hovering. How is the PM to know it is switched off?

'Volcano, what volcano? I was strangled for a witch.'

A male voice from across the room calls out, 'My pal and I were burnt for buggery. And ken this – we'd do it again.'

The man in the next bed glowers. 'Battle of Dunbar. Piss off.'

His neighbour ruptures all known hospital rules by dragging deeply on a clay tobacco pipe. 'Press-ganged for your English navy. Jumped ship and forgot I couldn't swim.'

A pale young woman calls from the other side. 'Hunger did for me, missus. There's a lot of it about.'

The PM spins on her heel and accosts the Secretary of State for Style, demanding an explanation. But he is suddenly busy, murmuring with considerable urgency into a portable telephone. He seems not to notice the PM at all, averts his eyes, and walks rapidly off the ward. Shaken by such cavalier treatment on the part of one of her favourite minions, she turns her wrath upon the two doctors. What, she demands, is the meaning of this charade?

Is she disappointed? asks Danny Dalziel, with unfeigned concern. If she'd like a bit of variety, there's a ward upstairs full of Covenanters and consumptive Romantic poets (fighting like cats and dogs).

And if it's disaster victims she wants, offers Dill, try the corridor outside. It's crammed to the rafters with people who never made it off the health service waiting lists. Plus some really prize-winning industrial injuries.

The PM appeals to the film crew. 'I hope you're getting all this. I want it all for evidence.'

'Sure thing,' grins the camera-woman, jingling her Rococo earrings. Shona, ever ready to turn her hand to something new, has discovered a fresh creative outlet. 'Maybe I'll really learn to work one of these some day,' she whispers to Dill.

'I suppose there is some explanation,' blazes the PM.

'Of course,' replies Dill. 'History has come to get you.'

CHAPTER SEVEN

ATOP A FAVOURITE DEPARTMENT store of the Edinbourgeoisie, the tearoom is crowded, as any other of its ilk, with lunching ladies. The aromas of cakes and coffee, the sound of Christmas shoppers' chatter, do not vary in any respect from those to be found in similar establishments anywhere from Aberdeen to Plymouth; the only difference is the view of sloping gardens, and the massed spires, turrets and gables of the Old Town, rising up the ridge towards the Castle rock.

But when Albanna and I step out of the lift, the room falls silent. With a symphony of clatters, thumps and rustles, the plastic carrier bags full of plunder slide from laps to floor. Fashionable hats and flowery headsquares are doffed as their wearers rise, revealing the formidable battle-plaits and tattooed foreheads of our senior commanders.

'Hail to the Queen Invincible!' they cry, in the guttural accents of our ancient Mother Tongue.

'Cream cakes for all!' commands Albanna. 'Then down to business.'

This meeting of the tribal High Command takes less than an hour, even allowing for the obligatory poems of ritual salutation between the generals and their Chief. As our officers disperse to carry out their orders, someone tugs Albanna by the sleeve.

'Excuse me, missus.'

Outraged by this audacious act of lèse-majesté, Albanna turns with baleful eye upon its perpetrator, then breaks into a smile.

'My dear, how delightful to see you again!'

It is the erstwhile Debriefing Centre tea-girl (and ex-waitress at the shooting lodge), now employed – as the lettering on her overall reveals – in this highly respectable department-store tearoom.

'What brings you here?' inquires Albanna, all regal graciousness and charm personified.

'You. I think you're brilliant.'

Albanna preens. 'Just doing my job.'

'Well, I want to help you do it. I'm only working in this dump because I knew you'd be coming here today.'

Albanna stiffens. 'And how did you know that?' She turns to me, and mutters out of the side of her mouth, 'Breach of security. Spies in the ranks . . .'

'Unlikely,' I reply. 'We only chose this place three hours ago.'

Is that a slightly disappointed droop to the queenly visage? Is she to be denied her extra *frisson* of fun? No interrogations, no torture sessions, no ruthless purges of the troops?

The waitress tugs at her sleeve, exasperated.

'Don't you remember when we first met, and you showed me how to do the face paint? I told you: I can See Things. Long before they happen. So I knew last week where I'd find you today. I had plenty of time to come through from Glasgow and get a job on the spot. No problem. They're always desperate for staff here – the pay's diabolical.'

Albanna brightens. 'You can See Things, can you? An invaluable skill, and one sadly neglected in this barbarous age. Benighted fools. They seem to rely instead on primitive mumbo jumbo, like market research and opinion polls. Pathetic, really.'

The waitress nods. 'Aye, it makes you weep.'

In our tribe, second sight comes as naturally as doodling a Pictish V-rod-and-crescent motif on the nearest rockface. You might say it's something of an ethnic trait. Indeed, the Dumnoni and the Votadini were prone to make rude jokes about it.

'At last,' cries Albanna, throwing her royal arms wide, 'one of My Own People!'

'Well, maybe on my granny's side. The rest is mostly Italian. They don't See Things. But they do make great lasagne.'

Albanna's eyes light up. I can almost hear the mental gears engaging.

'Blood of my blood! I have kept my promise. I have come to save you!'

'Well, I don't really need much saving, thanks, except from this effing coffee machine!'

'You know, we could use a bright young woman like you in our operation. Couldn't we, Gwhyldis?'

Typical Albanna. Whenever it's time to stick the queenly neck out, it's not 'me' or 'mine', it's 'we' and 'ours'.

'I'm sure she'd be an asset.'

Albanna points to the lettering and logo on her young friend's overall. 'I suppose we shall have to purchase your freedom from your present masters.'

'No problem. I've already quit. Do I get the job?'

Outside the Royal Infirmary, the Prime Ministerial minders and helicopter crew wait on the grass of the Meadows, watching the occasional wisp of vapour rise from Arthur's Seat.

'Longish visit for an out-of-London disaster,' muses one.

'Lots of jolly photo opportunities – and only one camera crew to cover it all.'

'Time's getting short, though.' A glance at the digital watch. 'According to the schedule, she's due back in London at 17.00 hours to address the Corporate Freedom League on the new Morality in the Media Bill. Better send someone in and tell her to get her skates on.'

But as their emissary nears the door, Drs Dillon and Dalziel emerge.

'A message for you from the PM,' says Dr Dillon. 'She and the Secretary have gone directly to the disaster site on the last ambulance run.'

The minder looks at the time again, starts to protest. Dr Dillon raises an admonitory hand.

'And she says to tell you to cancel all engagements for the rest of the day. The security forces will be organizing her return transport when the time comes.'

'That's very odd . . .'

'Apparently,' interposes Dr Dalziel, 'some sort of high-security matter has arisen.'

'What?'

'All we know', murmurs Dr Dillon, with a quick glance from side to side in case some foreign power should be lurking behind the trees in Middle Meadow Walk, 'is that a suspicion has arisen that this eruption . . . may not be the result of . . . natural causes.'

'Terrorism?' splutters the helicopter pilot. 'That's impossible. How could anybody reactivate a dead volcano?'

'Ask me no questions,' says Dr Dalziel.

'And I'll tell you no lies,' says Dr Dillon.

An hour later, panting from her climb up Arthur's Seat, Dill joins me, as arranged, in Albanna's burial chamber. Her next gasp has nothing to do with overworked bronchials.

'Gwhyldis! What on earth have you done to her?'

It's the PM indeed, but looking even more ironclad than usual. Still breathing, but rigid as a waxwork, her face with the blankness of a latex puppet's mask.

'A bit of surgery,' I reply.

Dill is aghast. 'You never . . . !'

I hasten to reassure her. 'Oh, not your sort of surgery, Dr Dillon. One of my own subtle, bloodless procedures. Something like a psychic tonsillectomy: I've extracted all her moral certainties. Not a moment too soon; they were becoming quite malignant.'

It is just after lunch in St Andrews House. The uppermost layers of the Scottish Office hierarchy have been hastily summoned. When all the mandarins are in place within the meeting-room, the doors are closed for a suitably impressive interval, then suddenly thrown open to admit the Secretary of State for Style.

'There has been a Cabinet Reshuffle,' he announces. 'And I would like you in Scotland to be the first to know. I have assumed the duties of Prime Minister.' He smiles, modestly, while the stunned silence gives way to gasps, the gasps to stifled giggles, the giggles to a pattering of applause. 'And I would like to introduce your new chief . . . Ladies and gentlemen, the Colonial Governor.' Albanna steps forward and takes a bow.

They look – to the extent that senior civil servants can display emotion – somewhat startled.

'But, with respect, madam, the . . . ah . . . previous incumbent . . . ?'

'Gone South. A reward for services rendered. New appointment still under wraps. I am sure the PM will make the public announcement as soon as she is able . . .'

They all know who Albanna is. Some, indeed, have shaken her hand at official receptions. And although there have been rumours – nothing solid – that the Venerable Celt no longer enjoys the status of Downing Street flavour of the month, they shrug their shoulders at this last turn-up. There have, after all, been even odder appointments at St Andrews House . . .'

'As is my privilege,' Albanna continues, 'I am co-opting specialists from outwith Civil Service ranks to join the team. My colleague here, for example,' Albanna brings forward her new Glaswegian acolyte, who has exchanged her waitress's uniform for a well-cut skirt and a no-nonsense bow at the neck, 'will be in charge of all financial and statistical forecasts. The others' – she indicates the row of poker-faced pinstriped career-women behind her – 'you will come to know and appreciate in due course.'

As one, these newly co-opted advisers smile at the mandarins, exposing teeth filed to perfect points and lips stained carefully with woad. From their slim leather attaché cases they bring forth Filofaxes and bronze daggers.

'I'm sure we shall all enjoy working together,' says Albanna. 'Meeting adjourned.'

Albanna is deeply disappointed when the new Prime Minister – speedily elected by his colleagues down in Whitehall upon receiving the news of his predecessor's inexplicable disappearance – declines her invitation to visit his former chief in her place of captivity. The ritual gloat, she explains, is the most important part of a Proto-Pictish victory celebration – even more amusing than fighting the battles that come before it. Is he absolutely sure, she asks, that he wouldn't care to march down Princes Street in a triumphal procession, with the old PM bound in chains and trotted backwards on a mule to receive the jeers and peltings of the populace? He has but to say the word – she could set the whole thing up in a matter of hours. She appeals to me, standing by her side, for confirmation. Why go to all the trouble of beating your enemies, she asks, if you don't have the fun of kicking them when they're down?

He pleads pressing business in the southern capital, where the Minister for Patriotism and other colleagues wait eagerly to form the new government.

'Frankly,' announces Albanna, 'I think you're afraid to face her, even now.' She turns to me. 'You know,' she confides, 'I'm beginning to wonder about his leadership potential.'

'Perhaps we should help stiffen his character,' I muse aloud. 'Send him on one of these newfangled Outward Bound courses.'

'Very far outward,' agrees Albanna, reaching for him with a gauntleted arm.

A weekly squash game and a fondness for modish Army Surplus jackets do not make the former Secretary a match for our peculiar combination of powers. He is easily incapacitated and allows himself to be led away, too dazed to notice where we are going. We bundle him into a police car, thoughtfully commandeered by our own cavalry, and head back up the hill to Albanna's old burial chamber. There he finds the deposed PM and the ex-Colonial Governor, backed against a wall of runic inscriptions, receiving a lecture from Dill on their government's most heinous crimes.

'This nice man,' I inform the twins, who look up from their jigsaw puzzles to study this new captive with a critical eye, 'is an important arbiter of public taste. He has many contacts in show business and the arts.'

As one, the girls rise from the floor and launch into their tap dance. The erstwhile Secretary raises his voice above the syncopated clatter, demanding to be released.

'All in good time,' I say.

But the mopping-up operation has barely begun. It will take all my cosmic energy to gather in the key members of the ex-PM's retinue – the loyalists, the front men, the fixers. I had better tap into the nearest stone circle to recharge my batteries, or I will be worn out before I clear the Cabinet.

'You'll have to drive me out into the hills,' I tell Dill.

'Take my police car,' says Albanna grandly. 'I'm sure my Mistress of Horse can find me another.'

Dill hesitates. What about the twins?

'They must be getting tired. Perhaps we should take them home first.'

Impossible, I tell her. We're leaving them here, to keep an eye on our guests.

'What? They're only babies!'

'Those are my chosen daughters,' I remind her. 'I think they'll cope.'

The girls have positioned themselves in front of our captives and immobilized them with a basilisk stare. Then: *tappety-tappety-tap-tap, tappety-tappety-tap-tap*. Albanna, Dill and I exit fast, before we are transfixed in turn.

On Cairnpapple Hill, the winter light is blue and scalpel-sharp. I can see most of Albanna's old realm, and the lands of the tribes that lay around it. The stones from the old circle are long gone but the holes remain, and they are full to the brim, invisibly, with all the materia magica I need. No one has tapped into them since the last time I was here, when I came to collect the wherewithal to organize Albanna's Long Sleep and Great Awakening. But exactly what I do, and how I do it, is nobody's business but my own. Dill, at my request, waits in the car. She doesn't mind: I'm sure she has a few professional secrets of her own. Anyway, the day's as cold as the Grey Goddess's supernumerary nipple.

When Dill and I return to the burial chamber, we soon have it crammed, as planned, with famous – and infamous – faces. The twins are getting a little overexcited. They have been dancing for hours, with their little tap shoes striking sparks off the stone floor. But it is understandable: they have never had so large, or so illustrious, a captive audience. I suppose it might have been picturesque if I had roped and gagged the PM and her gang to allow them to struggle valiantly – in the mode of old silent-movie heroines – in their bonds. But we wizards have subtler and more stylish methods. And I think the girls look rather sweet. They've figured out at least six new routines by now. Practice makes perfect. Besides, it never hurts to tire them out a bit – paving the way for hot cocoa and early bed all round.

What our reluctant guests think of this performance I have no idea. The least they could do would be to applaud, and gladden a doting mother's heart. Never mind – they aren't exactly famous for their artistic sensibilities. And it's no use their trying to curry favour. I know what I have to do.

'Right, girls, you can hold off now. That was magnificent.' It takes them a few moments to stop spinning. I turn to Dill. 'Ice cream for the ballerinas, I think. Triple scoops. And I'll meet you at Morningside later.'

'Where are you going?'

'Off to tie these maidens to a metaphorical railway track.'

Whatever should I do with them? Looking out from the top of Arthur's (sorry, Albanna's) Seat, my gaze falls upon the tower block where I lived when I first arrived here. The sunlight glints off the electrified fences. I am tempted by an easy option. What if I deposited the whole crew in one of the abandoned flats in my old homestead? Plenty of room, once they cleared out the rat droppings and used syringes. Imagine poor old hard-pressed Mum in a faded pinstripe pinny, trying to control her band of hard-drinking, womanizing grown-up sons. All those big, strong louts and not a job between the lot of them. Of course they have only themselves to blame: those plummy accents put people off. Think the world owes them a living. Wonder what the old girl would do when the tax collectors and the bailiffs start coming round? They'd try to talk their way out, of course, say who they were and all, but no one would believe it. A few days on cheap carbohydrates and that Standard Class drinking water and their own Undersecretaries wouldn't recognize them.

A pleasant scenario. I'm sure Dill would enjoy it. But somehow I don't think they'd be quite safe enough, even if I stationed a pack of particularly surly Votadini thugs in the flat next door to keep an eye on them.

Maybe I should revive one of the very old tricks of my trade, and turn the whole lot of them into trees. From trees comes wood, from wood comes pulp, from pulp comes paper. From paper come top-secret documents embarrassing to the government. From top-secret documents come scandals, unless someone gets there with a mechanical shredder first. We Celts are firm believers in the transmigrations of the soul: the sequence would display a certain poetic justice.

But in the end, I go back to the game-plan I thought of in the first place. What with all these Amazon armies streaming over Holyrood Park and Princes Street and Goddess-knows-where next, we have a few vacancies back in the Old Country. Not to mention a chronic labour shortage. So I do in reverse what I have done for myself, Albanna, and the Proto-Pictish Maidens' Militia: move the PM and her minions back to where we came from.

I'm sure they'll adore it, once they get used to the mutton fat and the lack of indoor plumbing. The climate is bracing and the opportunities are boundless, for those unafraid of a little honest hard work. As long as they don't expect any bleeding hearts to give them free handouts, I'm sure they won't starve. If they show enough initiative, they will undoubtedly be able to make something of themselves. And those who revere Traditional Moral Values will find it close to paradise: one step out of line wins you a starring role as a human sacrifice at the next harvest festival. You can't get more traditional than that.

I foresee a great future for these people in the past. Especially the Leader. Who knows – with her natural talents, and that inborn air of command, she might very well forge a new political career. Now that Albanna has shifted operations to the present day, I understand there's a vacancy as Queen. As long as she learns to mud-wrestle, she has as good a chance as anyone.

With this pleasant task completed, I seek out Albanna. She is standing on the battlements of Edinburgh Castle, declaiming some blank-verse epic to the roaring, ecstatic throng. They do not seem to notice that it is in our Mother Tongue – or that it scans so badly that I cringe to hear it. I elbow my way through the mob. It would be easier if I didn't have to struggle past Dill's old friend Shona and a band of devotees, who have painted their faces in a fair imitation of our own. They smile beatifically as they pelt the Queen with freesias, tulip heads and rose petals.

'Hold your horses,' I say to them. They don't hear me, wouldn't listen if they could. Ah, youth!

By the time I reach her side Albanna has finished her declamation, and is acknowledging the tumultuous applause and appreciative ululations.

'You do have a way of pulling the crowds,' I tell her.

'I haven't lost my touch. Have you disposed of all of Them, as per orders?'

'All absent and accounted for.'

'Excellent. Now that you've got that little obstacle out of the way, there is nothing to stop me taking over.'

'Don't be ridiculous,' I tell her. 'That's the last thing your people need. You were supposed to rescue them, not land them deeper in it.'

Her eyes narrow. The little serpents incised above her eyebrows coil and threaten to strike.

'Look at them,' she scowls. 'Hundreds of different tribes, opinions, creeds, factions, conflicting interests. You know as well as I do, they'll be at each other's throats by tea time if someone doesn't intervene and keep them in order.'

'That's what you said the last time,' I remind her. 'And that's why your burial mound is crammed with treasure from your grateful friends in Rome.'

She opens her mouth, closes it, opens it again.

'You're fired,' she says.

As I explained to Dill, I was conned. I really believed – more fool I – that just this once Albanna was going to see reason, and do what I told her.

Except for the fact that she will exhort them in blank verse instead of little monetarist homilies, I don't suppose the general public will notice much improvement. Not as long as she manages to woo the Press, and persuade the money men to see things her way. And I shudder to think what she will do about that other queen. Challenge her to a horse race, perhaps? Winner takes the Crown? And which brand of Romans will she sell us out to this time?

'You've got to do something,' says Dill, as we fall – exhausted beyond the point of lust – into bed. 'Or nothing will really change at all.'

'I'VE got to do something? ME? Give us a break – I'm only a magician.'

My spell collection, I remind her, may be the best in the business, but there are limits. I might know how to change a fat cat into a thin mouse, but so what? Dr D of all people should understand – treating the symptom isn't the same as curing the cause.

'Can't you send her back where she came from?'

'Reverse transmigration isn't easy. Not unless she wants to go. And I'm afraid that, compared to our day, this place looks like Heaven.'

In the end, we made a deal: I'll figure out some way to put the brakes on Albanna, and she, Dill, plus several million other people, can do the rest.

Albanna, with a fine sense of history, has set up her headquarters on the Castle rock, in the old Fortress of the Maidens. Her off-duty Amazons lounge about the Visitors' Centre, cleaning their finger-nails with the points of their spears, breaking into souvenir short-bread tins with their double-headed axes, or puzzling over illustrated guidebooks, which they are holding upside down.

I suppose I am now *persona non grata*, with Albanna issuing the usual strict instructions to hound me off the premises or dismember me on sight. But these warriors don't frighten me: there isn't one of them I didn't personally put through her initiation rites. And if anyone tries to block my entry, I will simply transmute myself into a floral tribute, sent into Albanna by some favour-currying defence contractor, or her loyal fans in the Druidical Lodge.

But I am spared the humiliation of turning into a gladiolus; the

Amazons wave me through with nods, salutes and – in one particular case – a flirtatious wink. In her Operations Room, I find Albanna and two of her commanders kneeling on the stone-flagged floor, studying a vast array of maps.

'Ah, Gwhyldis,' she beams. 'You're late this morning. Having too much fun to get out of bed, were we?'

'You seem to have forgotten. I've been sacked.'

'Oh, that . . . Never mind. The heat of the moment . . .'

Heat of the moment, indeed. She's decided she needs me.

'We've been discussing strategy. I'd love to have your views.'

And no wonder. Those two epic heroines at her elbow are the salt of the earth, but endowed with considerably less brain than brawn. And I suppose her canny young Glaswegian friend has her hands full elsewhere, reorganizing the Civil Service. Albanna wants someone to talk to.

'It's the old debate. Do we go for territory or simply plunder?'

'You're joking. You've just taken over a realm many times the size of the old one. Haven't been in power as long as a week. And now you're looking for new lands to conquer?'

'My dear, it's irresistible. Do you have any idea of the military resources at our fingertips? The ingenious weapons? The size and splendour of the fleet? And we're not talking rafts and coracles. This is the big time.'

I might have known.

'And there are some very rich pickings. I've been up all night, getting briefings on the best of them. Look over there, for instance' – she points to a spot on the map of a land mass far to the south, and across a broad span of ocean. 'A paradise of endless sunshine, warmth and wonders. What a place for our new imperial capital!'

I bend and look closer. I'm glad I've learned to read the native runes. She's discovered Florida, and set her sights on Disney World.

'You may meet with some resistance.'

'You'll find a way to break it down. You always do. But you'll have to make it snappy. I want to launch a sneak attack before the month is out.'

Once again, the old girl has surprised me. I had no idea she'd get greedy again so fast. Swift action is called for. I make my excuses, something about an urgent need to read some entrails on Albanna's behalf, and go off for a marrow-freezing walk on the windy beach at Portobello. I find the sound of lapping waves very helpful when confecting plots.

It doesn't take long. Inspiration strikes. But I will need some help. I ring Dill from the nearest pay-phone, and ask her to round up her friend Shona. That's easy. Then I ask her to track down our old fellow-prisoner and Souk-trader, the silent but artistically gifted Ms L-O-V-E & H-A-T-E. This may not be quite so simple. But my lover is a genius when it comes to playing the Edinburgh news-and-gossip networks: she did it when she rescued the twins, and now she amazes me again. By the time the Number 15 bus has completed its tortuous journey from the shores of Portobello to the heights of Morningside, both Shona and Ms L-O-V-E & H-A-T-E are sitting on the floor, elbow deep in a vast bowl of Dill's hot garlic-buttered popcorn. I muscle in to eat my share before it's gone, and we get down to business.

Two days later, I report to Headquarters again. This time I find the maps rolled up in an untidy pile in one corner of the Ops room, and the floor covered instead with great sheets of computer print-out. A portly male lawyer crawls among them, reading aloud extracts indicated by the prodding spear-points of the two commanders, and inking in changes as Albanna barks them out.

'Just like old times,' she grins, when she sees me. 'I'm drafting edicts.'

'What happened to the great invasion plans?'

'Postponed. A few domestic matters need some attention first. The natives seem to be getting restless.'

I'll bet.

Albanna extends a foot, prods the legal gentleman's pinstriped backside. 'Read out those last ones. I'd like to know what Gwhyldis thinks.'

He could save himself the trouble. No matter what I say about them, she'll never listen.

They don't impress me. The usual nitpicking inventory of What Is Not Allowed, and the gruesome list of punishments for those who Go Ahead and Do It Anyway. Some deeply unfair new taxes. The return of slavery, that fine old traditional institution. And a compulsory military draft of all females under the age of fifty-five.

'Well?' demands my Queen.

'As you say, Albanna, just like old times.'

And, speaking of old times, I tell her, I have just come across a fascinating ancient document that I think she will find of considerable relevance and interest.

'So let's see it. Hand it over.'

'It isn't in my pocket. It's carved on a standing stone. I found it this morning when I was walking through the glen behind the Salisbury Crags. Barely an arrow's flight from your old burial chamber.'

When we arrive on the Crags, sped there in Albanna's commandeered police car, sirens wailing, we find Dill and Shona waiting for us. I have allowed them plenty of time to cover the surface of the little papier-mâché monument with a plausible veil of greenish-yellow lichen.

'One of the earliest decipherable inscriptions in any Celtic tongue . . .' breathes Shona ecstatically.

'And what a remarkable state of preservation!' Dill exclaims. I nudge her. No need to be too effusive.

'Look!' I point to the carving of a great scaly-tailed dragon that twines about the text. It has a human head, and wears an imposing crown. The features are unmistakable: an unnervingly accurate caricature of Albanna's former rival – our late, great PM.

'I knew she'd rise to the top once she got there!' I exclaim. 'Some people are simply destined for greatness . . .'

Albanna glares at me balefully.

'Read it!' she snarls. Like most warriors of her day, she has left that particular skill to wizards, scribes, and other weaklings.

Shona, ever the Celtic scholar, explains with pretty deference that it is actually a Gaelic translation of some earlier Proto-Pictish text, but none the less represents a breakthrough for scholars, since no primary sources in Albanna's own Mother Tongue have yet come to light.

'READ IT!' roars the Queen.

'There may have been Queens before,' intones Shona, peering carefully at the carved script, 'and there . . . will, I think it is . . . fortunately . . . no, that must mean probably . . . be Queens again . . . But all are obscured, removed from our songs, by the triumphs of she who came by . . . sinister, no that's mysterious, manner . . . to our tribe, in the year of the terrible . . .' she stops.

'Get a move on . . .' commands Albanna, through clenched teeth.

'Sorry,' says Shona. 'I can't. That's all there is. The rest has been worn away . . .'

Albanna looks at me. I look at Albanna.

'She pulled it off!'

'The bitch!'

'Wiped you right out of the tribal tradition, so it seems.'

'Not if I have anything to do with it.'

'What do you mean?'

'We've got to get back there and stop her. Can you manage it?'

I refrain from any interesting discourses on the technical and metaphysical problems of rewriting history. But now it's time for me to enjoy a little ride on my own high horse.

'Can I do it?' I echo. 'Can I do it? Can the great priestess Gwhyldis, who shot you through time like an arrow, send you back again whence you came? Do you doubt my skill? Do you forget all that I have done for you – here, and back there? Do you think I am some mere apprentice, capable only of the minor magicking of frogs into princesses, and other parlour tricks?'

'Oh, Gwhyldis, never. How could I? Why, you know . . .' And I let her grovel for a bit. Spilling out queenly praise like a nice hot shower.

'All right. I'll do it.'

'With all my warriors, of course . . .'

'How else, O magnificent Albanna? It looks like you might have a battle on your hands when you get there . . .'

She signals to one of her commanders, who pulls out a great ram's horn and blows a mighty blast that summons the troops. Once again, the Amazon army swarms over Arthur's Seat.

'Let's go.'

I give Shona a comradely kiss on both cheeks, then fling myself at Dill for a more serious embrace. For a moment we stand there, just looking at each other.

Then we all ascend, in single file, to the burial chamber. Albanna stands at the crest of the mound, arms folded across her chest, counting off the warriors as they climb down into the tomb. Finally she descends herself, pausing only to say, 'Now the first thing I want you to do when we get there . . .'

I step up to the opening, then kneel down, carefully lowering the stone to seal the gap. 'What did you say about "we", Albanna?'

Then I murmur a few words of power, and they are gone.

Slowly, silently, Albanna and her Amazons sink back into the smoky depths of lost myths and all-but-forgotten legends. But the traces of her formidable rival upon this later age are not so easily eradicated. The marks are there for all to see; the prints of hobnailed stilettos cut deep into the soil. The lady may be out of the game, but she has not been wiped from the collective memory bank. Far from it.

For down in the homelands of her tribe, in the leafy lanes of southern suburbia, in the smart converted warehouses of the London docks, in the glass-walled boardrooms of the new money and the dark-panelled club-rooms of the old, there are a few faithful acolytes who keep the flame alive. They turn their collars up against the chill, and mournfully scan the ancient epics for any trace of their long-lost heroine. And in the cold, dark nights, they tell this legend to their children:

That she and her great warriors lie sleeping, in a hidden chamber deep within the earth, far below some demolished factory, decommissioned nuclear power station or abandoned mine. There they rest, snug under a blanket of sanctimony, with their double-edged swords clasped in their hands and their ancient financial gospels pillowing their heads. And some day, a trumpet will blow, and the great Queen will rise again. And, with a mighty roar, she will summon her troops to pull their socks up, and will come to the aid of her own people when the tables are finally turned against them.

But not if Gwhyldis has anything to say about it.

HEARTBREAK ON THE HIGH SIERRA
Fiona Cooper

'Pure fantasy, great fun . . . This book seems to have it all' – *Alison Dilly*

'A lesbian Western, with plenty of lust in the dust . . . hilarious and sexy' – *Gay Times*

'I heard there was a place a woman could hang her hat up without any trash bothering her.' This is the wary hope of the enigmatic world-weary reporter, Helena Stanforth, aka Typewriter, aka Fools-rush-in, as she keeps moving west, 'always a little ahead of what they like to call civilization'. Hounded from Chicago to Crazy Man's Coolee, all her dreams are at last realised in Kimama, the valley of the butterflies. Here, Suzanna LaReine and her pistol-packing outlaw crew wisecrack along in harmony, until trouble comes in the form of Darknell van Doon, 'an oil-tongued reptile pirate in a fancy suit'.

Heartbreak on the High Sierra is a lesbian western in true spaghetti tradition, bubbling with thrills, spills and suspense; a story that begins with a cataclysmic storm and builds up to a rip-roaring climax; a romance where love and laughter reign supreme, and all the baddies bite the dust.

BROKEN WORDS
Helen Hodgman

'Stylishly bizarre . . . funny and poignant, a vivid evocation of the cruelty and beauty of life' – *Shena Mackay*

'It is all Tom Sharpe – or even Dean Swift – and it is loathsome. And fearless. And very funny' – *Evening Standard*

As the sun rises and sets on Clapham Common, Moss, her young son, and lover Hazel scrape by on the DHSS. Then Moss's ex-husband tips up and Buster and Beulah and baby (courtesy of the milkman's sperm donation). And finally, the Bogeyman with chipped junkie eyes.

Helen Hodgman lives in Australia. Virago also publishes *Blue Skies & Jack and Jill:* 'It's ferociously funny to the end. Immensely stimulating, like a small dose of strychnine' – *The Times*